I0788482

WAYFINDING SAVAGE

and Other Stories by
ELISA LOVE STOWELL

Elk Meadow Press
Evergreen, Colorado, USA

ISBN: 978-1-962526-00-5 (hardcover)

Order copies of Wayfinding Savage and Other Stories at the Publisher's website:

https://sites.google.com/site/toddledermanauthor/

Or scan the QR code to visit the website and tour other titles.

For *La Famiglia*

CONTENTS

Foreword

A few years after I became an extended member of Elisa Love's *famiglia* by marrying her sister, I watched a documentary supposedly depicting two of the world's greatest kayakers. These men, the voiceover announcer said, had decided to run what is perhaps the world's most notoriously difficult river: El Rio Biobío in Chile.

The film opens with the two men in their kayaks running an extreme section of whitewater. They round a rocky bend as the camera zooms out to reveal the big picture: a scene far more terrifying than the section the kayakers have just navigated.

The whitewater they successfully ran leads to a not-quite waterfall. The two kayaks are approaching the top. The drop is about fifteen times the length of their boats, maybe 150 feet. Below them, sheets of cascading whitewater flow not more than thirty degrees from vertical.

Oh. My. God.

"Oh my god! That's the river Elisa ran in Chile!" I shout, though no one is around to hear me. Rivers run through most of Elisa's stories. Some of these fictional tales are filled with a hefty helping of her life's truth, such as Wayfinding Savage. Others are mostly autobiographical but seasoned with a *soupçon* of fancy. Yet, among these stories she never gives us more than mere hints of her skill at navigating whitewater. From my view, it appears as though Elisa, in these stories and in her day-to-day demeanor, consciously minimizes her mastery. Her reasons are her own, but I suspect they have something to do with reading the river and deciding the safest course is to avoid currents that could lead to a crash against rocky walls.

One river, however, used to consist solely of torrents leading toward rocks. El Río Biobío. To my knowledge, Elisa has never written an account of her journey. My version of the story comes from Elisa's telling, but is brief, lacks detail due to my poor memory, and probably partially wrong. My apologies.

By her mid-twenties, Elisa had run rivers in Colorado, Utah, Idaho, and Arizona. She led trips for a commercial rafter, and in 1980 the company owner made her an offer. He had heard of a fantastic river in Chile, the Biobío, that featured miles of whitewater. Would Elisa be interested, he wanted to know, in an all-expenses-paid trip to Chile to run an exploratory trip on the river? If her journey went well, they would begin offering commercial trips to raft the Biobío.

All expenses paid? Sure!

While making arrangements for the trip, she learned of another company that also wanted to make an exploratory run. Then, other river rats wanted to join. Soon, a total of six professional rafters would comprise the expedition. That sounded good. Safety in numbers.

Six rafters, five men and Elisa, gathered upriver from Santa Bárbara, Chile. They inflated, assembled, and rigged six rafts and began their journey.

"It was 200 miles of whitewater," Elisa explained.

One boatman dropped out after the first day. Another flipped his boat and left the party. Two others also flipped, and the river catapulted their rafts into boulders, ripping apart pontoons on both boats. One more rafter was badly injured and had to leave, as the others had, over land. None of the five experienced boatMEN were able to finish the run on the river.

But Elisa did. News of the expedition's difficulties had traveled downriver. So, as Elisa approached Santa Bárbara with her boat intact, townspeople were lining the river's banks, shouting and cheering for the boatwoman who had successfully navigated El Rio Biobío.

I don't know any further details of her Biobío trip. She never told me how she set up on a series of five rapids rafters would later name "Royal Flush". Nor do I know how she managed the rapid called "Lava South" because it is reputedly more difficult than its namesake in the Grand Canyon. During her days of running rivers, Elisa rarely drew attention to her skills, so naturally, she left those details out of her tale. But after watching that documentary and seeing film of that river, I know one fact for sure, and I hope readers remember this as they wend their way through her stories. When she ran rivers, Elisa was not merely a 'good boatwoman'. She was a fucking beast!

—Todd Lederman

Note: In 1992, Chilean authorities closed most of the whitewater portion of the Biobío to make way for a massive reservoir and hydroelectric generators. The "One-Eyed Jack" and "10 of Hearts" of the "Royal Flush" series of rapids now lie under a concrete dam.

Wayfinding Savage

PROLOGUE

SHE TOSSED BACK the bed sheet. Getting up, she felt around the floor for her robe. The floor was cold in winter. Careful not to arouse her sleeping mate and a house full of animals, as well, she wrapped the yellow flannel robe around her body. The chill made her nipples rigid. A fire in the wood burning stove would be a fine thing, she thought. On the stove she placed a kettle of water for tea. The kettle sizzled over the heat. She sat at the table and pushed her black mane out of her face. She opened her diary and wrote:

> Your photo fell out of the pile.
> I picked it up with a smile.
> I looked at you, you smiled back.
> It's not wistful love that we lack.

ONE

Theressa Rose could see the dust from a car coming up the dirt road to the house from her second-story bedroom window. The old Victorian mansion lay in a thicket of cottonwood trees with their branches hanging over the roof.

Late autumn winds forced the trees to release their leaves and lay down a golden carpet over the shingles, hiding all evidence they had suffered from lack of attention for twenty years. Theressa felt her heart settle. A calm transpired over her body as she lay in bed. She felt satisfied that her three granddaughters, who were in the car coming up the road, would see the house covered in leaves. Perhaps the girls would finally realize their grandmother meant to die, entombed in the aura of this season's most glorified change. In fact, she would be sure to mention to them, to wet the leaves down before they wrap her body in them, for the smell of wet leaves after a rainfall was, by far, her most favorite fragrance on the earth. She did not want her relatives and friends to suffer the indignity of the odor of death. She preferred a more heavenly scent, rejuvenation of the return to the earth. When her body entered the ground, she wanted her loved ones to smell the freshness of starting over again. In her prayers, she asked God, in light of her kindness to all living beings, a special favor, to turn those leaves that would enwrap her body into the color of blue ash, floating into the abundant turquoise sky.

The car rounded the bend and slowed down in front of the house. There was a patina of dust over its crimson red paint job. One of the women got out of the car and leaned over to use the side view mirror to put on lipstick. She wore a very tight skirt which forced her to stick her butt out. It looked as though she was trying to catch some fresh air after the long car ride.

The three granddaughters walked onto the porch. They talked as they walked up the steps. Chimes rang with the breezy winds. They went up to the screen door in the front of the house. Maria knocked. Nobody came. She turned to look out onto the barren landscape. The wooden planks creaked under her cowgirl boots. "It sure looks lonesome out there," she whispered to herself as she stared.

They walked around the balcony to the back of the house. Recollections of childhood filtered through their talk. As they stopped to look at the ruins of a barn, the aroma of cinnamon and chili caught their attention. The scent came from the open kitchen door. Maria and Cassandra looked inside. In front of the stove, over a boiling pot of chili, stood Meg in a frock that hung off her as though she had forgotten to take it off for at least ten years. She was stirring the chili.

"Hey Meg, how much chili are you making?" Angelina asked as she hugged the old woman. The woman turned her body as though it had been void of free flowing movement for many years.

"Girls! Girls! Good to see you." Maria and Cassandra rushed forward, each placing a kiss on her forehead. Entering the outreached arms, Angelina could smell the scent of garlic on her fingertips.

"That chili smells like you put in the right spices. Have you got it strong enough for the old lady?" Angelina asked. She unwrapped the scarf from her neck and gave her hair a tussle. "The winds are kicking up around here. I suppose she thinks the spirits are cleansing the air."

"Quit being so smartass. You college educated people have no sense of poetics. How would you know what the spirits are doing when you sit at the computer all day?" Meg lifted her nose into the air and sniffed, "I think the spirits in the chili are strong enough for that gal. She's been waiting in bed all day for your arrival. Come on. Put your coats in the laundry room."

The women dropped their coats onto the washing machine and followed Meg through the living room and up the stairs. She knocked on the door.

"Please, come in," the women heard her say in a faint voice.

Meg opened the door. In the brass bed, next to the window lay a woman, well groomed, sitting upright on the pillows. She was in her nineties. Her face, surrounded by fine white hair pulled back into a braid, glowed. She wore black. A pearl necklace traced the high neckline on her dress. Her dark eyes revealed a genuineness and refinement, expressing compassion from within. The wrinkles around her eyes carved a smile as they entered. She had invested much time in her appearance that day, but from the askew lipstick on her mouth, one could sense it was a struggle to appear so sculpted.

"My girls! Come give me a hug."

The room smelled of burning sage. The aroma came from a ceramic bowl on the bureau. In it lay a smudge stick made from sagebrush. Next to the bowl was a wooden cross about six inches high. The figure of Jesus was intimately carved into the wood. The women knew the scent meant grandmother had just performed a purification ritual. The indigenous root served as a symbol of transition. Theresa Rose often said burning this sacred herb helped the spirits to enter hers and often guided her toward knowledge obtained in an altered state of consciousness that led her to take measures that would effect a healing. She claimed it helped her to see clear through the cross. Thus the cross became a crossroads as well as a crucifix.

The women moved to the bed. They bathed her in respect.

"Grandmother, you look beautiful," Maria insisted.

"Thank you. God has asked that the younger woman in me make an

appearance."

The women surrounded their grandmother with hugs that were as familiar to her as the hugs she had once received at the end of a full day of fishing. For every fish the girls had caught, they had given their grandmother the equivalent amount of those affectionate gestures. The bigger the fish, the longer the hug. Theressa Rose caught herself in memory of bygone years and long ago summers.

"Sit down on the bed. I want to have a special day with you. I do not ask for much more time to live, so I felt this was the proper time to reveal the diary your mother left. I found it among her things a few years ago. She was a very private woman and she might have felt disturbed at the intrusion. However, I also know your mother always sought the truth in life, so I think she would want her daughters to know the truth about her."

Silence tenderly illuminated the room. Beyond the silence, a distant thunderstorm rumbled in the hills. The scent of impending rainfall meandered through the window. The branches beat against the tin, shedding more leaves onto the roof. A spillway of rain descended from the organdy sky. The thought passed through her, 'Perhaps the girls won't have to wet the leaves down.'

"What diary is this, Grandma? I didn't know mother ever settled down long enough to write," balked Cassandra. The sisters knew there was still a charge of hostility in Cassandra's heart whenever anything came up about their mother. They knew that once she had her own children, the hostility would wane. Theressa Rose, however, could not let her boldness go unnoticed.

"Cassandra, you are only being hard on yourself. Your mother was there for you much of your childhood. When your father died, she had to go back to work. Please, try to understand. Destiny does not enable one to prepare for the future. Granted, she had to go on the road for work, but how much did you really suffer? Perhaps at the university, one pays homage to suffering, so the spirits of happiness must leave."

Cassandra looked down. "I'm sorry. I just wanted to be with her."

Theressa Rose said "I'm getting cold. Meg, would you make a fire in the stove? Let's make some coffee and sit by the fire. Maria, you read from the diary. My voice tends to cramp up these days — but, I'm always ready to give an opinion or two."

She touched Cassandra's hand and gave it a long, hard squeeze. Angelina moved to help her grandmother out of bed and signaled Cassandra to help carry her downstairs. The women were careful not to drop her.

TWO

The light in the living room danced in shadowy movement. The evening sun was disappearing. The storm clouds blocked out the sun every few minutes. The women's faces were cast in light and then darkness, rhythms of the moody storm. The warmth from the fire massaged all feelings of the responsibilities towards life outside this home. Angelina sat on the couch and poured coffee for her sisters. Theressa Rose declined. She had given up coffee many years ago. Old age had caused the jitters that coffee once did. The sisters drank while she sat in a slumbering trance. When they finished, they put the cups back onto the tray and sat back into the chairs, moving their bodies around the pillows for optimum comfort. The old lady awoke. She pulled a book out of her pocket. The women were ready to hear about their mother.

Theressa Rose passed the diary to Maria. She looked at the cover awhile and turned the book over in her hands. She then opened the book carefully, as though the spirit of Isabele Ranchera grew from within the lines of the written work

"I feel like I'm doing what I shouldn't," Maria said as she looked up at the grandmother. She closed the book and turned it in her hands.

"I must say, although you feel this way, you all will benefit greatly from this reading. Ignorance cannot help in the healing." Theressa Rose spoke in her usual pedagogical manner, an accent that had aided her authority when she had worked as a school teacher in a small school on the border of Colorado and New Mexico.

Maria opened the book. She cleared her throat and began to read.

*   *   *

When Isabela was born, the midwives held out their hands to receive the newborn. She moved into the new world with gentility. As the midwives checked her over for signs of health, they raised their eyebrows. The baby had very large feet. They wrapped her in the blanket, commenting that those feet would bring her good luck, and passed the newborn over to the parents. The father cried with joy as he held up their firstborn child.

The baby opened her eyes. She looked at her mother. She then looked at each person in the room, turning her head from face to face. The elders knew then that this was a special baby.

Born in Trinidad, Colorado, on a small family ranch nestled in a canyon beside a river, Isabele grew up a happy child. From her cradle, she listened to the birds sing in the cottonwood grove, and by the time she was two years old, she had mastered the sounds of a meadowlark, a crow, an owl, a canyon swallow, and a rooster. She lay in the cradle and from her sweet lips came the singing of a swallow. The cats always napped around the base of the cradle wishing the baby was actually the bird they thought they were hearing. They purred.

At the age of four, she took over the use of her mother's bike. Those feet made it easy for her to learn balance. In one afternoon she taught herself to ride down the dirt road, kicking up as much dirt as she wanted. She laughed as she skidded into the cottonwood tree, the dirt flying into her face as the tire swirled to a stop. Her mother stared at her from the balcony. She felt graced by God for having such a lovely child.

As a young lady, Isabele took up the lariat. She had watched her father lasso the young calves at branding season. His speed impressed her. She practiced on an iron bull with horns, but found it dull after a few tosses. The cats watched from the railing of the fence. Preparing the rope for another toss, she suddenly turned toward the cats. She ran after them, swinging the rope around and around. The cats jumped off the fence and ran for the barn, fearing their fate. Through the barnyard, around the pond, and into the house she and the cats played team roping. When she became good, the cats decided to hide.

During the summers, she spent most of the time balanced on a wooden barrel, floating the river, and swinging the lariat to catch the reeds that grew along the banks. The rope flew as if it were as light as dried dandelion seeds floating into the air. It landed in the tall willowy plants and she pulled on the rope as hard as she could. The loop snapped shut around a single reed and the wooden barrel stopped in the middle of the river.

With those feet, Isabele tried balancing on all modes of transportation: inner tubes, logs, even homemade rafts. After swinging that rope ashore a thousand times, she could stop on a dime. She would make her parents laugh by dancing tango with a rose in her mouth on her homemade raft. She reached the end of the raft, kicked up those lanky legs, and twirled around and around.

Her parents called her Isabele. Her intimate friends called her Beau. She was as beautiful as a spring tulip. She had the strength of a bear. In her prayers, IsaIsabele would say "Honest, God, I really don't mind these big feet. I just wish people would not notice their size."

During junior high, the neighboring boys joined her and formed an exclusive baseball club. They used the extra baseball field at the schoolyard and played after school. They did not really want the formality of competition, they just wanted to hit a few balls around. When the time came to elect a captain, the boys poked their fingers into her. "Rose Beau, you need to be our captain."

While playing on the field next to Isabele, the coach of the school's official baseball team would turn his head from his own team's action to watch Isabele at bat. She would always spit into her palms. She kicked up those big feet and stirred up the dirt, as if it were instinctual. She swung the bat and the ball sailed into the bright cyan sky and sailed about fifty feet past second base. She always put it there.

"What a hitter!" Coach would mutter. When the school, as usual, came in third place at all-state championships, he felt truly bitter. "If only the school allowed girls to play," he complained to the principal.

As Isabele became more conscious of appearances, she cried on her mother's shoulder. "Isabele," her mother said, "those feet have brought you good luck. You have the hooves of a 'caballo'. Someday, those feet will save your life."

THREE

When Isabele reached the age of nineteen, she started at the university a few hundred miles away. She would have started after high school, but her father fell ill for two years and needed Isabele there to run the ranch. She was apprehensive about leaving her father, but he insisted he was feeling better and that she needed to be educated.

"Just learn how to think. That's all I ask," her father had said.

And that is just what Isabelle did. At the university she began to think about abortion rights, segregation of the sexes, diversity, AIDS, a part-time job, and a new boyfriend. In her prayers, she began to address the God essence as the Goddess/God essence. And she asked the celestial partners for a little time off. Life wasn't as simple as it had been in her childhood. In the spring, she was given a reply. "Go to the river, go to the river, go to the river," the voice chanted through her.

She responded by hooking up with a few people who were planning to raft the Green River. She packed a dry bag full of clothes, threw it and a water jug into her 1973 VW convertible bug, and headed west to Utah.

In the canyon at the put-in point at Gates of Lodore, she met her group, elders of the river who had acquired the spirit, the dance of the water. "Masters," they called themselves. Masters are people who have let go of enough control of their bodies that they can perform stunning acts of movement with water in very small kayaks. Masters had little social decorum. They were more attuned with the forces of Nature than to the forces of political correctness. They had no particular use for clothes. Each had a unique relationship with the water. If the Masters were represented by an animal spirit, it would be the river otter. For Isabele, these people were kindred spirits.

She had the time of her life when she learned to kayak. The masters taught her. She was convinced it was the only way to know the soul of the river. Year after year, the masters showed her the way downriver. At first, she swam most of the rapids, but after a few seasons she kayaked the waves with the vibrancy of a Master.

"You have to bear down, get a grip, and go with the flow, or you lose your ass in the big hole," they would tell her.

The masters invited her to return each season to run the river. She found that the "tribal" connection to the water balanced out the demands of her university education. Each summer she returned. The masters called her "Bodacious Rose" because her style on the water could not be beat.

She met her future husband on the river. At first, she mistook him for a river pirate, those people who perform acts of wizardry to keep common folk confused. He was a big man and about as brazen as any man comes. A tiny silver pig dangled from his ear. He wore a bandana over his head. He laughed louder than any man, and his heart was bigger than any other man's she had met.

"Isabele, ask me to get married," he said. "Whenever I asked a woman to get married, I always had bad luck. Two failed marriages. I want this one to work. Besides, when we are together, each of our lives are like two rivers flowing in separate canyons. I know we want to flow together so let's meet at the end of the canyon. Like a confluence."

She fell in love. One day, while floating the Grand Canyon together, she got on her hands and knees in the sand. She pulled him down to her. He put her hands on his heart. She asked him to marry her. "Of course!" he said. She grabbed his beard and planted a juicy French kiss. They were married. She committed her life to him, but there was an unspoken understanding between them. Isabele was as independent as a woman could be. He knew when she needed time to think about the rhythms of her life, the river was still her sanctuary. And he appreciated her freshness when she came back from the river. Besides, he loved her exactly the way she was, big feet and all.

Soon, the babies came. They were made from a love deeper than the canyons of all the waters in the world. It was a time of great nest building. Three girls, that's how many they bore together. Isabele felt great satisfaction. She grew fully feminine. Breastfeeding accorded her a greater understanding of womanhood. She had always thought of her breasts as an androgynous appendage with no value until she felt the fullness of motherhood.

FOUR

The spirit of the Masters called on her to return to the river. Isabele had been away a long time. She decided to raft a group of women downriver while her girls stayed with their grandmother.

Isabele asked a few friends to join her on the river. In those days, the women's movement had become bogged down with rhetorical bullshit. She asked these women to share a few days in a place where they didn't have to feel the invasion of prominent political views, feminist in-fighting, or male-bashing.

"I just want to be in the freedom of our sensuality, goin' downriver, basking in the sun, and drinking a few beers," she told them in seductive invitation.

Two rafts and nine women arrived in the evening at the Westwater Ranger station on the Colorado river in Utah. The river looked like milk chocolate. It must have rained heavily upstream because only flash flooding could cause the river to become this color. They unloaded the equipment from the truck. They pumped up the rafts before dark. When there was no light left, they sat by the river on their rafts and talked. They talked of their childhood, they talked of their men, and they talked of their experiences on the water.

Isabele had invited her psychologist. She was part Cherokee and part Ph.D. She held sessions in a teepee behind her house, and Isabele had depended on her interpretation of the world for a while. When the psychologist moved away, Isabele discovered she had depended on her a little too much. She hoped to kindle a friendship by asking her onto her territory — the river. To her surprise, the psychologist had a fear of water, but Isabele reassured her that she would be on Isabele's boat.

Isabele rose before the sun to begin rigging the boats. She organized the equipment for inspection by the ranger while the other women made breakfast. Already, Isabele felt a sense of serenity, of women working together to get the job done. Usually, when a group of men and women go on a raft trip, there is much commotion about division of labor among the sexes. She always viewed the put-in point at the river as a study in dominant baboon behavior, each male trying to outdo the others in the telling of river adventures.

As she bent down to review the medical kit, she heard, "Good morning," and looked up. The river ranger was standing behind her. She noticed how well-ironed his government uniform looked.

"Good morning. I've got the equipment ready for inspection."

"Are you the trip leader?"

"I am," she said as she looked into his eyes. Frosted sapphire. Icy blue. She always had trouble diffusing through the aura of people with eyes that color. But his eyes seemed friendly.

"I'm Cody Reed." His mouth slid into a smile. IsaIsabele grabbed onto the word "Reed," bringing forth memories from her childhood on the ranch.

"You must be new here," she said.

"This is my first season."

They checked the equipment together: enough life jackets, rescue ropes, spare oars, a port-a-potty, ash can, and medical kit.

"You're well organized. This is great. I like people who make my job easy."

"I like river rangers who appreciate my work," Isabele responded with a dignity acquired through years of experience.

"What kind of group are you taking down?"

"I'm taking some women friends."

"You mean this is an all women's trip?" He beamed.

"You got it." Isabele wrestled with the buck knife tied around her waist. It had started to move towards her privates and she pushed it away. "Wow! That's great. Unusual around here."

Cody wanted to meet the women. She gathered the group, thinking he was going to lecture them on river safety. Instead, he expressed his delight in their bravery. They all looked at each other. His patronizing behavior was about as weak as a third round of coffee with the same grounds — inviting aroma, disappointing taste. The more his efforts to impress mounted, the more the women tried to ignore him. They just wanted to be left alone. Isabele knew, however, just how rare a scene this was. She took him aside.

"Look, we're just lookin' to have a good time. We are not out to make some kind of feminist statement like, 'Women can rock the boat as well as rock the cradle,' got it?" IsaIsabele put her hand on her hip and swaggered to one side. She tossed her black mane out of her face.

"You're funny. You really are. I'm just paying you a genuine-leather, heart-felt compliment. That's all. What's your name?"

"Beaudacious Rose." Isabele couldn't help herself. Teasing this man felt natural and easy. Revealing her most intimate nickname amounted to an invitation of friendship. Yet, she had to stick to the premise of the trip. No infestation. "My given name is actually Isabele."

"Isabele, I'll remember that." He turned and walked back into the building. Isabele watched him leave. He had beautiful legs, she thought.

"Okay, we can finish rigging the boats now," she called to the rest of her friends.

When all the equipment was tied down, the women donned their life jackets with varying degrees of ease or awkwardness. Isabele beckoned the psychologist onto her raft. "You'll probably have the same feelings I did when I entered your teepee," Isabele said as she turned to the psychologist and tugged the straps on her life jacket. "Usually, you're the one to beckon me into vast unexplored territory. Now the situation is reversed. This should be charming."

"Isabele, just don't flip the boat. This is a big step I'm taking. My life is in your hands."

"Well, my life was in your hands for a long time. Just relax."

The rafts floated away from the shore. Isabele waved to the ranger, who was standing on the river bank. He waved back. He watched the rafts move downriver until he could no longer see them. Isabele rowed in circles to loosen her muscles. A serenade from cliff swallows echoed melodically across the canyon. The blazing heat softened these women. The boats floating in and out of waves softened these women.

"Don't get too lazy," Isabele warned. "The true rapids are yet to come. Skull Rapid. It always psychs me out. There is a big hole in the middle. I've managed to avoid it the past twelve years. But last year I ran on the right side of the hole and ended up in the Room of Doom. At high water, rafters sometimes don't get out of it for hours. One group had to be helicoptered out of the place."

Isabele figured this was as good a time as any to indulge in river tales. "The Room of Doom has left boaters stranded. It's a small canyon, about one hundred feet across. Boats'll smash up against the walls. Rowers have to shove and heave with all their strength to move the boat across a five foot high eddy line. Sometimes, in the late afternoon light, you can see the etchings of a side view of a skull close to the rim of this small canyon. That's why it's called Skull Rapid."

After a few hours on the river, the women grew hungry. They found a long, secluded beach. Immediately upon stepping on land, they tossed all their clothing into a pile.

"Aahh YES!" Isabele yelled as she rubbed her chest.

Lunch was simple. Finger food and no agenda. Tossing olives into the air, some women made sport of catching them in their mouths. Beautiful, full-figured bodies ran with the innocence of children at play, trying to retrieve those black airborne objects before they hit the sand.

One of the women noticed a kayaker paddling toward the beach. With no time to scramble for clothing, some women crouched in the sand while others stood solid in the indignity of the intrusion. As the kayaker approached, he took off his sunglasses. It was the river ranger.

"What's he doing here?" Isabele scowled.

He paddled up to the shore. "Sorry, ladies. Hey, Beaudacious, you forgot your buck knife. I thought you might need it." She remembered she had left it on the rock while changing into her swimsuit. Man, this guy has an eye for detail, she mused. She walked over to the kayak.

"You women look so relaxed. I'm sorry. I hope I haven't embarrassed you. This is the place to be naked." He handed her the knife.

"Thanks Cody. Actually, nobody is embarrassed."

Signs of irritation, however, were stirring in one woman. She was a lesbian, and her militant feminist views were often quoted in the local newspaper. Isabele respected her intellect. They had become good friends through the caretaking of Isabele's children. Their mutual concern for the welfare of the children rose above all bias toward gender preference. She had been in the line of fire so frequently these days, that Isabele had asked her to go on the trip for her health, to gather strength. She threw piercing glances at Cody, which Isabele thought were just a bit too hostile.

"Would you like some lunch?" she asked.

"Sure, if it's okay with everyone?" one of the women sauntered up to him. "It's okay with us as long as you don't mind if we stare at your ass," she said.

"Fine with me. This is an opportunity I can't pass up." He pulled off the spray skirt of his kayak, pulled himself up and out of the boat, then stripped down to his shorts. He thrust his shoulders back and stretched his arms, then bent down to touch his toes. He walked through the sand and sat by the food.

Lunch with Cody was delightful. He seemed to be designed by the Goddess/God to protect the wilderness of this area. He was a poet as well as an environmentalist. Isabele could tell he was an athlete from the salient definition of muscles. On the other side of his gregarious nature was a loner. He was committed to the preservation of this area and talked very easily for a long time. The women started getting restless.

"Hey Isabele," the lesbian said, "Get a hold of your hormones."

"Bev, I tried giving up hormones long ago. Why, are they getting in the way?" asked Isabele.

"Yeah, it's getting a little thick around here."

"Okay, I got it." She turned to Cody. "Cody, I'm glad to have had lunch with you, but we must get downriver." Isabele signaled the psychologist to bring in the boat's bow line, which they had tied to a tree.

"It was a very fine lunch," Cody looked at Isabele "I appreciate the hospitality from you women. You just can't turn down an invite to lunch with naked women. I've done my damndest to keep the testosterone from spilling out. I tried to give up that hormone long ago too." He let out a laugh. "Haven't had much success, though."

Isabele shook her head. She got up and dusted the sand off her burnt sienna skin. As she moved toward the boat, he moved toward her.

"Can I run with you ladies? I took the day off."

"Cody, you are a wonderful man. But, I billed this trip as an all women's trip. As trip leader, I must stick to my promise. Already, I sense this is just a little too heterosexual for one of the women. I have to take everyone into consideration."

"I understand." Cody winked in recognition. "Can I wait at Skull Rapid, to see how you run it?"

"'That's fair enough. But that's as far as you go with us."

"Yes, Ma'am."

Isabele studied Cody as he donned his gear and pushed from shore. He moved over the waves with the grace of a water moccasin. She had kayaked this water for many years. The spirit of adventure had not left her, but had been modified to accommodate the innocence of babes. She still loved to watch expert kayakers.

The psychologist had strapped the ice cooler onto their boat. She waited for IsaIsabele to get on the oars. Before they pushed off, IsaIsabele showed her how to wrap a bow line and then strap it to the boat. Isabele stood on the frame and wrapped the rope around her elbow, as fast as a cowboy could wrap a rope around the horn of a saddle while chasing a calf. Several times the psychologist practiced. They pushed off shore. The paddle boat was close behind. Two eagles circled the high cliffs. The water was cool enough to wash away the heat from lunch.

The canyon started to narrow. Black walls closed in. The water funneled into rapids and pools. Some waves were twenty-five feet high. Nice level, thought Isabele. The two boats shot through a series of rapids.

She shouted to the other boat, "Skull Rapid up ahead! We're not scouting. Water's too fast!"

Indeed, Skull Rapid was just downstream. Late afternoon lighting on the canyon wall made the skull clearly visible. Isabele rowed the boat to river left. She wanted to be in the slow water, so she could stand on the seat to study the flow.

"Oh good, Razor Rock is covered this year," she told the psychologist. "Hold on!"

The psychologist sat motionless. Isabele sat down and tucked the oars under her ass so she would not be tempted to use them until the river told her what to do. The boat moved toward Razor Rock and slid over it. She raised her leg and freed the left oar, then took a single stroke to keep the bow headed downstream.

The boat pivoted. "Damn!" Isabele shouted. The oar had bounced off the rock and broke loose from the oar pin. She had no left oar. Where was it? Nowhere to be found. She took a stroke on the other oar. The boat was headed toward the big hole. She spun and spun and spun the boat in a circular motion to keep it from going over the hole.

The psychologist, sitting in the front of the boat, rode onto the lip of the big hole. Her eyeballs swelled. She was paralyzed. Isabele kept turning the boat. Once past the hole, they were past danger.

Cody appeared right in the middle of the rapid. He went straight for the hole and did a few endos, on purpose.

Isabele watched. Behind him, she could see the oar thrashing around in the Room of Doom.

She yelled. "Cody. CODY!" She shouted above the roar of the rapid. "COOODY!"

He looked around.

"MY OAR'S IN THE ROOM OF DOOM!"

Without hesitation, Cody pushed against the currents and paddled to the other side of the big hole. While he tried to cross the eddy line, she saw that he was tangled in a rope.

"Where did that come from?" she wondered. Mystified, she stood up and walked around the deck of the boat. The bow line was undone. Damn! She thought her friend had understood the technique.

The psychologist turned around. "That was a great run. I liked it from a 360-degree view." She had no idea what had happened. Isabele bent down and grabbed the rope. It was still coming down stream, all thirty feet, until Cody got caught in it. She could see he was struggling. The rope wrapped itself around the body of the kayak. She dropped the rope. If she pulled on it, she might tie him into one big knot. He pulled the rope away from the kayak and lifted it up and over his paddle. He wrestled the rope like it was a snake. His arms flailed to and fro and the rope was finally free.

"No way!" She watched Cody. He was now in the Room of Doom, retrieving the oar. He crossed the eddy tine with the oar laid across the spray skirt. He moved around the lower lip of the big hole and over to the raft. Isabele stood. Shaking her head and grinning as she held out her hand for the oar, she realized opinions must change. This was an awesome boater!

She bent down to take the oar. "Thank you. Really, thank you!" She looked into his icy blue eyes. They glowed ultra blue in intensity. "You deserve a kiss," she said and bent down even further. Going for the style of kissing that was a sincere expression of appreciation, she put her lips onto his. His tongue hurled into her mouth by some celestial incentive. Isabele moved back. He grabbed the back of her neck and pulled her forward. She started to melt inside. She had better stop.

She pulled back again.

"Hey!" Beaudacious. You offered a kiss and I took you up on it!" he beamed.

The moment seemed frenzied with stunning acceptance of friendship over the roar of Skull Rapid.

"See you later," Cody yelled as he pushed off the raft. Isabele watched him as he glided downstream. She watched until he rounded the corner of a canyon wall.

"Out of sight!" she laughed. "That is one ballsy dude."

She popped the oar back in and waited for the other boat to float past. Then, she pushed off the canyon wall and continued the journey downstream.

While floating on flat water, the psychologist came out of her trance and turned to Isabele, "You mean, we popped the oar at the top of the rapid? I thought you staged that!" The psychologist felt gratitude. Her boatswoman had lost control, yet she had no idea she should be afraid, so she wasn't. On the canvass of her mind, the experience painted the meaning of Zen.

By late afternoon, the women floated out of the canyon and found their campsite. That night, they danced naked to the beat of a drum under the stars. The canyon was black. Some women drank tequila. Some swam in the water. All celebrated.

FIVE

The next summer Isabele came with a different group. It was the ranger's second season. At first, they greeted each other with formality, but after some consideration, they hugged each other with a formidable exchange of heart.

The equipment passed Cody's inspection. The boats were about to pull out from shore when Isabele leapt from the boat. She walked over to the ranger station and knocked on the door. He appeared at the door with no shirt on. "Hey, it's a heterosexual scene this year. You want to paddle along? We have plenty of food," she offered.

"I would love to go, but the head honcho from the district office is coming today for inspection. Damn!" Cody sighed.

"Damn is right. I'll see you next year." She turned to leave, but stopped, cocked her head around toward him, and looked him in the eye. "Thanks for saving my oar." He winked in recognition and said, "Absolutely. My pleasure."

The day on the river was wonderful. The passage through Skull Rapid was smooth for all boats. By late afternoon, they had floated out of the canyon. Several boats were ahead of Isabele's boat. She and her companion, Sue Falls, were in no hurry to find camp. The bullfrogs started to sing. The hot sun made them lazy. They laid on the pontoon of the raft, idly moving their feet around in the water. Isabele's dog, Yampa, slept on the dry bags.

"Isabele, I brought my bullfrog whistle," Sue said.

"Get it out. Let's make music." Isabele responded with delight.

She pulled out her whistle from the dry bag. It was a bamboo reed, attached to a rubber tube- When she blew into the reed, the rubber wobbled back and forth. Out of the end of it came the loud and clear sound of a bullfrog's mating call. Sue blew that whistle. At first, one bullfrog responded. And then another frog responded. And then another. Soon, the whole river was an orchestra of bullfrog mating calls.

Isabele and Sue laughed. They lured the bullfrogs downstream. They sang the Bullfrog Song. It went something like this:

The bullfrog call, it calls all.
So follow us. We're gonna have a party site.
Leave your roost. We'll sing to you.
Gonna dance into the night
And kiss you, too.

The women sang silly versions of the ditty for the rest of the afternoon. They sat up when they saw two men from the group running on the sandy bank. They were yelling for Isabele to row across river. She rowed. over to them.

"They're in our camp," they said excitedly.

"Who is?" Isabele asked.

"The Hatch group from Salt Lake City."

The Hatch group carried the Mormons down river. The boatmen were usually self-righteous, macho-motivated punks. Isabele rummaged through her dry bag and found her buck knife. She strapped it onto her waist. She really had no intention of pulling it out, but she liked the visual effect. She stood on the rowing frame and waited until the raft rounded the canyon wall. There they were, their camp set up on Isabele's designated site. As the boat came ashore, Isabele and Yampa jumped off.

Three guys were sprawled out on the sand. They were lying on their backs, with their feet buried in the sand.

"HOWDY. Who's the head boatman here?" she asked.

"I am."

She looked down at the voice and walked closer to him. She stood directly in front of him. She saw his privates hanging out of his cut-off jeans.

She knew the intent of this display from watching other commercial boatmen. It's called "turkey necking". The boatmen let a little piece of cock hang out while they're rowing. They claim it "turns the women on." They receive a better tip at the end of the trip. Isabele had always thought this behavior was left over from the Freudian phallic stage. Most men would exit this stage around age six. But some boatmen extended its life expectancy. She scanned him over, showing no offense at his crudity.

"I think we have a problem here," she said.

"We don't have a problem. You have a problem," he retorted.

"We were assigned this campsite by the ranger. You've made a mistake."

"Well, you're the one who has made the mistake. We're not moving."

By this time the group from both raft trips had gathered around. Isabele's lawyer was among the group. He was attracted to the contentious nature of the scene and moved closer to Isabele. He crossed his arms and started rubbing his chin.

"I have a permit signed by the river ranger," she said.

"The guy told me to take any campsite I wanted," the boatman replied.

"Bullshit!" She let irritation slip through her cool.

"Hey, Bitch. I've been running rivers for three years—"

"Three years? Why you're just a punk. I've been running rivers for fifteen years, but that's not what matters here. I want to work a win-win compromise. Obviously you are not going to move because you have set up camp. I understand that. My people are tired and we don't know what's available downstream. Campsites may be taken. This campsite is big enough for both groups. Why don't we compromise? We can set up camp up on the hill."

"No way!" He was still lying on his back. Isabele was tempted to take out her buck knife and do something about his privates hanging out.

The lawyer broke the hostility. He pulled on her arm. "You're not going to appeal to this person's sense of fairness. We don't want to stay here anyway." He put his hands on her shoulder. "Come on, Beau."

"Keep the campsite!" she yelled. As she turned to leave she saw Yampa take a dump in a bush next to the boatman. The boatman bolted upright in sheer disgust. She mused, 'If litigation can't take care of a problem, poetic justice sometimes does.'

They found a campsite downstream. While pitching the tent, Isabele saw a kayaker paddle ashore. "The river ranger wanted me to apologize for him," the kayaker said. "He accidentally gave you a campsite he'd given to another boatman. He's sorry."

"Thanks," Isabele replied, "I already found that out."

That night, she and two other women decided to make formal apologies to the other group. They put on their best river dresses. One woman wore a tight purple leopard skin skirt with matching gloves, and nothing else. She moved her long hair over her bare breasts. Another woman wrapped a scarf around her torso, leaving her ass exposed. And Isabele wore a shredded dress that left one shoulder bare and a lot of thigh exposed. They walked over the hill and down into the Mormon camp.

They sauntered up to the boatmen. The Mormons stared, openmouthed, at the procession. Isabele stopped in front of the "cock of the walk."

Isabele smiled. The women stood beside her. "I want to apologize for our conversation. We were informed by a messenger from the ranger station that he had given the campsite to both groups." The procession then turned around and sauntered back up the hill, leaving the group indubitably silent. Laughing all the way back to camp, they felt a sense of fairness, flesh for flesh. The battle of the sexes continued.

That night, the group celebrated in the light of the moon by diving off the cliffs into the warm water. After the trip, Isabele stopped by the ranger station. Cody was in the garage, working on equipment. Word had already reached him that there was a savage woman loose on the river whose dog had shit in a camp.

"Am I in trouble?" Isabele teased Cody from her truck as she pulled up to the garage. He laughed.

"Yeah, you are." He came over to the truck and opened the door. He pulled her out. "I want to talk to you." He pulled her into the garage.

Actually, she wasn't sure if she had done something wrong. It was legal to have dogs on the river, and she couldn't help it that Yampa had left a mess near the boatman. He pulled her over to an inflated raft sitting on a trailer. He turned to face her. When she looked down, she saw a hard-on building in his pants. He went to give her a kiss.

"Cody," she put her hands to her heart. "I'm really honored, honest. But I can't do this. I have another life." She gasped for air. She had to get out of there before she melted. She knew the feeling. His passion became embarrassment.

She took a step back. She had never met a man so forward with affection.

"I'm sorry. I don't know why. I don't know you very well, but the first day I met you, well, I just couldn't help myself."

"Oh Cody, You're a magnificent man, but I'm committed to another." They walked out of the garage. She put her arm around him. "You're a good friend. I hope you know that."

He changed the topic. "You sure had that boatman crying. What did you do to him?"

"Nothing, I even apologized to him."

"He couldn't stop talking about how savage you were. I'm sorry for the mixup — on two accounts."

They walked to her truck. Cody opened the door for her. She got in and put her hands on the wheel. She started the ignition. She sighed. They looked at each other. They kissed affectionately. Nothing more.

"I gotta return to my babies."

"You have to go home. I know."

SIX

Autumn. Isabele became pregnant with her fourth child. It was a tiresome pregnancy. She stayed in bed the last month. Her family supported her. In spring, she delivered a baby. She was overjoyed when a boy came out of her belly. The midwives took him away. He had complications.

The next few months were spent in the hospital, trying to save the life of the baby. Mistakes were made by doctors. Mistakes were made by the parents. A minor malfunction of the throat turned into battle after battle of infections, indigenous to hospital. The baby died at the age of one.

The Catholic priest came into her hospital room. Isabele had been asleep for two days. When she awoke the priest was standing by her bedside. "Would you like your baby baptized?"

Isabele stared at him. "What do you mean? Why would I want him baptized?"

"I'm sorry. The baby didn't make it."

Isabele sent the priest away. She cried in hysterics. Tears fell upon the earth and shattered into bits of frozen grief. The doctors had taken the baby and cremated it, deciding it was best to keep her from viewing his death.

How shameful of them. She had wanted to see the baby, dead, so she would truly know he had decided not to stay. His ashes were the only testimony to his birth. Since she

had not actually seen the body, she did not believe he was
actually dead. This made her CRAZY!

SEVEN

She wrote to the Masters that she would not be coming
to the river that year. She wrote the same thing the next
year and the year after that. She had taken to soloing across
country by horse. She traveled to the farthest hinterlands.
She traveled by night. She spent days and days, years and
years, on horseback. And when she knew she would only
find happiness inside the chambers of her own heart, she
was lost.

She was in a remote canyon in the Sierra Nevadas. She
sat on her horse in the moonlight, staring out over the rim
of the canyon. She saw the American river in the valley
below. They trotted down the canyon path. Moonlight
blinded her. She believed she was reining the horse down
the trail, but Isabele was taking the horse over a three
hundred foot cliff. The horse pulled its head around and
chose its own path. Her horse carried Isabele with swift
speed to the bottom of the canyon by the river.

Isabele looked into the river. It was blacker than the
other side of the moon. Which way do I go? she wondered.
The horse walked up and down the river. Was she to stay in
darkness the rest of her life? She got off her horse, sat on a
rock, and began to cry.

Moths began to appear. Flourescent green gel in the
veins of their wings reflected the light of the moon. They
flew above and around her, encapsulating her in their
movement. Hundreds of glowing moths flew to the river
and spread out like a landing strip, creating two parallel
lines, and lighting a path two hundred feet across the river.
She and her horse walked the path, through the water,

between the moths. They lit the way for Isabele to find her way back to her loved ones.

EIGHT

The next season, Isabele returned to the river. She brought her women friends. Alejandra was a mountain mama who had grown up on the Mexican American border. She had a lusty Tex Mex accent. "Where's this river ranger that you've talked about?" she asked as they rigged Isabele's boat.

"He's not here this week. He's away on government business."

"Too bad," Alejandra sounded genuinely sorrowful.

Two boats pushed off shore. Sorona, a sister rafter, was at the oars of the other boat. She had Rachel and Starlight Risk on her boat. Isabele took Alejandra and Laura on her boat. Laura was a hippie chick who was always smoking a pipe. She offered the pipe to Alejandra.

"Just to make peace," Laura insisted. So the women smoked the pipe while floating downriver. They passed it over to Rachel. Rachel was a photographer and a friend of Isabele's. She did not know anyone else. She took the pipe, smoked it, and passed it over to Startlight Risk. She was a transplanted L.A. city chick, a strict vegetarian and always well groomed. She declined. She handed it to Sorona. Sorona was happy to partake. The women were together in peace.

It was a muggy afternoon. The run through Skull was very successful, in fact the most exciting ride Isabele had ever rowed. The canyon was casting burnt sienna reflections into the brown Colorado River. The sun dripped over the cliffs. The air was hot and still. The cicadas were rubbing their bodies, creating their distinctive mating call. The sound emerged intermittently through tamarisk, those feathery old-world trees that had taken over the beaches, crowding out nearly all indigenous flora. This sandy beach was small, just big enough to provide camp for the six women.

They were excited by the run through Skull Rapid. As they stood in the warm river, they threw mudballs at one another until everyone was covered. Laughter ripped the stillness. The women were smearing mud all over each other. Mud balls were flying across the water.

Alejandra threw a mudball at Isabele. She moved her body to catch it by bending back and sticking her belly out. The mud ball splattered against her belly and slid down her pussy.

"That was so fucking amazing. That hole!" exclaimed Alejandra. "Skull was just too much."

"Yeah!" yelled Isabele "That was one gigantic hole."

Isabele took a handful of mud and rubbed the front of Laura's body, making circles around her breasts. Alejandra tossed another mudball at Isabele. Everyone was having a great time except Rachel. She was standing in the water, watching.

Isabele bent down and scooped up another handful of mud. She walked over to Rachel. She started with the face and moved mud down the cheeks and onto the neck. Rachel was silent. Isabele moved the mud down the belly and down the legs.

"There you go, a good cleansing!"

Starlight Risk didn't want to get her hair wet, so Sorona picked up a bailing bucket full of water and poured it over her head. She pushed her into the water.

Starlight wailed her disapproval.

"Hey, Starlight. Everyone needs a bath," Isabele laughed.

Isabele dived into the water, then came up for air. Alejandra hurled another ball at her. "No more mud. I'm done." Another ball flew through the air from the hand of Alejandra. "NO MORE MUD!" She dived under the water again. She swam under the branches of a huge cottonwood trunk, about eight feet in diameter.

The bark had been stripped from the trunk by the water when floating down the canyon. It had been at this place for many, many years.

The fat branches hung into the water. Isabele swam in and out of the branches. The women started to rinse off. Then, they set about making camp: basically, one cook stove, a box with pots and pans, and a cooler. Alejandra and Isabele climbed out of the water and onto a rock. They laid their bodies on the rock and roasted in the remaining afternoon light. Heat beat into their bodies. Quiet prevailed.

Isabele raised her head and stared out into the canyon. She gazed at nothing.

"It seems when I come on the river with a heterosexual group, it's the men, who upon reaching shore want to set up camp immediately. And I mean immediately. They move briskly just to find the right sleeping spot. When they have found just the right spot, they declare it as theirs by putting their life jackets on the spot. Those who think they are going to get laid that night put the life jackets farther away from the camp kitchen. I can just walk down the beach and know who's thinking about zooming whom."

"I guess that comes from being a river slut, hey woman?" Alejandra asked with her head buried in her folded arms.

"Probably so. Once, so long ago... Hey, Alejandra. I have something to ask you," Isabele lowered her head to indicate need for intimate conversation.

"Lay it on me."

"On the drive over, Rachel and I were discussing my son, the circumstances around his life. She told me I needed the death of my son in order to grow up.

"Now, you and I are the only mothers on this trip. I have come to you and you only. You would know in the most intimate way. I'm upset by that remark. What I want to know is, should I be?"

Alejandra dropped her jaw. "What a painful thing to say. How horrible of her to say that! It's about one of the most cruel, callous things I have ever heard. Why did she say that?"

"1 don't know. At first I thought it was because I wouldn't be her girlfriend. She wanted too much of my time. Then she said she was attracted to people who are suffering. She likes to photograph people that way!" Isabele sighed. "That made me even madder, because I had thought she wanted to strike up a genuine friendship. But, as it turns out, she wanted to prey on my suffering. Pretty damn gross."

"How long have you been friends?"

"Since my son was three months old. She asked if she could photograph me and him together in her studio. I said okay, and our friendship went from there. She has always been nice up until now." They lay in silence. "I wonder if she resents that I've gotten my strength back. It's been two years. I'm done crying."

"You may never be done crying."

"I know. Just before this trip, on Thursday, I took his photograph out of my wallet. I thought this needs to be an end of an era. Then, Rachel hurled this insult. I just can't imagine what another learning experience for her friends would be like." She sat up and made quote signs with her fingers. "I just wanted to cry."

"But, you didn't, did you?"

"No."

"Good for you. That's just what she would have wanted, that Anglo bitch. What did you say to her?"

"I just looked at her. I couldn't believe it. I told her that even though she perceived me as being irresponsible because I was once "too happy" to be a mother, I am, nevertheless, a very responsible person, and I have taken on much more responsibility than she will ever be able to experience. I also said I wasn't mad at her. That was a lie. As trip leader, I just wanted to keep the group dynamics pleasant. But I'm merely trying to survive."

Alejandra broke in, "I know my love. I'm so sorry." She put her arm around Isabele. "Don't worry. I'll take care of it."

Dinner was being prepared. Isabele threw her buck knife to Starlight who was going to cut the vegetables for the salad. Alejandra picked up an empty five-gallon jug of water and set it between her legs. She started to beat on it. Sorona was telling raunchy jokes. Rachel was making spaghetti. Laura smoked her pipe on her sleeping pad.

"This knife is too small for me to use," complained starlight.

"Hogwash. It's those damn fingernails," said Isabele. Starlight threw the knife onto the ground, "I'm not doing this anymore."

Alejandra noticed the bewildered look on Isabele's face. She stopped playing the drum. She sauntered over to the kitchen, swaying her toosh in exaggerated gestures. She walked over to the knife, picked it up, blew on it, tossed it into the air, bent down, and caught the knife again before it hit the sand. Isabele smiled.

"I'll do this. This job ain't no sweat for a Mexican like me. Cucumbers are our specialty."

Isabele walked over to the kitchen. She leaned into Alejandra. She looked to see where Starlight was before she spoke. Starlight was down by the boats.

"Had I known a woman could be this inane... Put her in front of a computer any day, but no way she can survive in the great outdoors. There are no conveniences."

"No," said Alejandra, "put her in front of a raging bull. I think she's had too much sand in her hair today. Must've set off some sparks."

"How could any woman want to be so physically inept? Forget about asking her to tie the boats up. Or even help carry any equipment." Isabele walked to the cooler. She pulled out a bottle of tequila, opened it, and took a sip. "Let's celebrate. Safe passage through Skull. Safe passage through life." She handed the bottle to Alejandra, who took a sip.

"To all the great mothers of the world!"

Alejandra passed the bottle to Sorona. She swigged a gulp. "To the next great lay that I'll have."

Laura took the bottle and took a sip. "I toast the trip leader who got us through Skull. What a bronc of a wave. I was really scared. The last time I went rafting, the boat flipped on top of me and banged my head. They found me unconscious in the river.

"Laura, hand me the bottle, please," Isabele said. She took another swig. "To Laura, who trusted me enough to come and show us just how brave and cool she is."

"That river ranger was a hunk, even though it wasn't the infamous Cody," Sorona said as she took the bottle from Isabele and drank away. "I think I'll just have a fantasy about him tonight. Too bad you ladies can't be there."

"We don't want to be there. We would be afraid to see what you might do to him," Isabele laughed.

"Isabele, what you said to him was so funny." Laura said as she puffed the pipe.

"You mean when he asked how long I've known all of you?"

"Yeah!"

"Well, I do go through a lot of friends. River rafting takes its toll. Not many survive season after season with me. I am known as the 'Velvet Hammer'. There's sound evidence why

I have that name. I replenish my friends every year." She laughed and so did everyone else. "What's wrong with telling the truth?"

"You took him for such a ride."

"Ah, he didn't mind. You should have heard our conversation when he was looking over the equipment."

"Don't tell," Sorona said, frantic that Isabele would ruin her fantasy. "I just want to imagine him all to myself."

"Oh, Sorona, you are such a river slut." Isabele ended the conversation.

Dusk set in. Dinner had been made, served, and eaten. Laura was at the five-gallon water jug drum, playing a Native American beat. She was pounding it out.

Her trance was interrupted by a thought. "I learned this beat from my ex-husband. He was a musician. He was also Apache. He had a bull's head tattooed on the end of his dick. Amazing sight when he had a hard-on."

"Tell us more," beamed Sorona.

"Oh no, that's as far as I go." She resumed playing the drum. Alejandra was dancing in front of Isabele. She smacked her behind to the rhythms of the drum beat. Everyone was a bit drunk. The air was electric with feminine energy. Lots of howling bursted across the river and against the canyon walls. The sky had turned the color of periwinkle. The glow of the unseen moon cast an omnipotent pearlescent light. Rachel took an innertube and floated in the warm water. The drumbeat grew more and more seductive. Alejandra started dancing without consciousness. Her body moved so sweetly, like the cherry tango on a hot cobbled street during Mardis Gras. She started to chant.

> "There's nothin' like family to make life
> grand. The blood of the blood of the blood. We
> are there for one another. Under any
> circumstances. I would die for my children as

my mother would die for me, as her mother
would have died for her.

*My brothers. They are the uncles of my children.
My uncles treat me and my children as my father
would treat me." Alejandra was in a serious dancing
and chanting trance. Her arms moved wildly
around and around. "My grandfather took in all the
children. Every summer. That's the way it's done in
our family. My aunts take care of any cousins when
the men leave. No matter who you are. When you
are family, there are no moral lessons that prove you
must grow. We grow as family. One plant. Growth
comes from unconditional love. A tragedy. Huh!*

"Does not prove maturity happens only that way. We are
the ancestors. We are the generation of pride. We are the
future grandmothers. Isabele, you loved your mother?
Come dance with me."

She pulled Isabele up. They twirled. Laura beat the
drum. They danced the tango. They howled. The other
women went to sleep. Starlight laid on her sleeping pad and
listened to the commotion.

The moon hung in the middle of the sky. The color of
the sky had become sapphire. Isabele, Alejandra, and Laura
sat on the rock. They admired the bright, plum moon.
Alejandra, still in a trance, chanted again.

*Wind comes forth from the fire. The image of
family. The clan creates energy. Wind stirred up by
fire. One's words must have power. Upon the
wellbeing of the family. As a king the father
approaches his family. Fear not. Mother gives freely
of her love. Father gives freely of his love. Their*

> *work commands respect. In the end, good fortune*
> *comes.*

Alejandra woke up from her trance. "The work has been done."

"Wow. You astonish me."

"That's because I'm so drunk."

"That was a great blessing."

"It is in your honor, Isabele, that I sing. For you and your family. We will call it Isabele's song. It's better than listening to the poor white trash with the nails."

Isabele needed to change the moment. "Hey, you see that cat walking across the cliffs." She pulled Alejandra down and pointed up to the cliff.

"No"

"It's right there." As she pointed, both she and Alejandra fell over on their backs. They giggled. Laura fell asleep. The earth was still. Alejandra pointed to a satellite nearing the Milky Way galaxy. The night air had a slight chill.

"I've never gone through the hole before. I've tried to avoid it for as long as I can remember. It was too fucking wild. Rachel got scared riding on Sorona's boat. Thanks for switching boats. You didn't have to do that."

"No problem, woman. That's about as far into Mama Earth's belly as we're ever gonna get. That wave just crashed over me. I'm feeling so fine. I'm so drunk. Tell me, Alejandra, how is it that you have three different children from three different husbands?"

"I don't know. The Latin doesn't know when to quit."

"Yeah. I know what you mean. I just love to make babies."

"No joke."

"Even the fourth one. He was such a challenge. Such a beautiful spirit. He was so ill for so long. I made a book for him when he was four months old. The doctors told me he was blind. I told them he doesn't focus on people who give him pain. They felt I was not being clinical enough to make a diagnosis like that...

"Anyway, this book was about a mother bird and a baby bird. They were either snuggling together, or feeding, or protecting one another. He tracked those drawings from north to south, east to west. He actually studied them. Then, the doctors and nurses came to the room, either to take blood or poke him with another IV. His eyes became paralyzed again. He had the control of a warrior."

"Yes, I know. He was so special."

They spoke until they fell asleep on the rock under the full midnight moon.

NINE

Beaudacious Rose had floated in and out of Cody's thoughts for many years. He was sorry he had missed her the last time she was down here. Something happened to her, he thought. He asked the masters if they knew. They only knew of her letters, which explained nothing of her absence. Cody asked boat group after boat group of her whereabouts. Nobody knew a thing. Eventually she disappeared from his mind, but not from his heart. This was to be his last season on the job. He was losing the environmental war. Mining had come to the area. Mountain bikers were tearing up more and more terrain.

The highway department had placed a gravel pit next to the ranger station. The air was dusty all the time. His health was impacted. He needed to move on. One summer day, there was a change in the air. Cody was at the bulletin board, writing down the water level of the river for the day. A truck pulled up, the dirt kicked up from the braking tires. Cody looked out from behind the board. He then stepped out. He stared. Isabele stepped out of the truck. His first reaction was shock. She appeared somehow beaten. He smiled, hiding his initial amazement when she moved toward him.

"Hey, Cody. How's it hanging?" she asked. They gave each other a hug. He squeezed her hard. Yet, he felt her essence was full of shyness.

"What has happened to you," he looked at her with wet eyes.

She told him this was her last time down the river. She had come to do it solo. She told him of her baby's death and of the years she had spent looking for peace.

"It's actually more complicated than I can explain. I spent a year in five different hospitals in two different states fighting for his health. All of it was senseless. The mistakes."

He listened with compassion. Tears welled in his eyes. She has changed. She no longer has a charge for me, he thought. The feminine splendor of the full breasted woman has left her body. She has moved into a more mature beauty. She talked of her children. He listened and yet he just wanted to hold her.

After a while, Isabele stopped the conversation. She went to her truck and pulled out the equipment. "You sure you want to do this alone?" he asked as he helped her pull out the raft.

"Sure do," Isabele answered.

"You can camp overnight at Little Dolores."

"No thanks. I only have the day."

She moved the equipment over to the bank. She had blown up the raft and was ready to tie on the equipment. She looked at Cody. "You want to inspect the goods?"

"No, I know you're organized," he said, wanting to inspect her. She moved with more grace than he had seen before.

She tied the equipment down to the raft and patted the boat. It felt good to be on the river again. She looked at Cody. "I'm ready to leave," she said defiantly.

"Alright, I won't go with you. The water flow is 23,000 CFS. you be careful."

"Thanks, Cody. I'll be fine." She pushed off shore and floated out of his sight.

She played with the oars, spinning the boat around and around. "Oh, Masters, what may I learn from the river this year?" she asked under her breath.

The boat floated down to the sandy beach where the women once had had lunch. That was a long time ago, she mused, those beautiful women catching olives in their mouths. A laugh escaped her. She parked the boat and tied the bow line to a tree. As she ate lunch, she watched several boaters float by. The river had become crowded over the years.

Among the flotillas, Cody paddled his kayak. He saw her from across the river, sitting on the beach, covered in sand. She could not see him, which made it possible for him to wait for her downstream.

After lunch, Isabele untied the bow line, wrapped it, and tucked it under her seat. She pushed off shore. She enjoyed being alone. She could hear the cliff swallows with more clarity. She was about to enter the top of the sequence of whitewater that led to Skull Rapid. She remembered what she used to tell younger kayakers.

"You have to bear down, get a grip, and go with the flow, or you lose your ass in the big hole." She summoned poise that prepared her for the big water. Downriver she went, swirling and tossing among the waves. Oh, the greatness of the canyon!

She heard the low pitch roar of the Skull. Coming soon, she thought. She sat on the oars. She followed the tongue of the rapid. The hydraulics have changed this year. All the water is going into the big hole! Before she had time to plan her next move, she was caught in the pull of the flow, moving into the hole. She tried to stroke out of the main current. But her strength was overruled. She was caught.

The water was sucking her into a fifteen foot standing wave. She turned the nose of the boat downstream. At the lip of the big hole, an unsuspected side wave reached up and pushed her boat askew.

"Damn!" Isabele shouted. The boat was beginning to flip sideways on top of her. Razor rock was behind her. She was about to be smashed. She kicked her feet into action. Jumped out of the chair. Scrambled up the nose of the raft. Feet aided in balance while she pounded them onto the frame of the boat's high side. She jumped so hard the nose plunged through the wave, then the whole boat settled into the main body of water. She had passed directly over the hole. The boat and she were still right side up.

"Hallelujah!" she yelled.

She looked around the boat. All the equipment was still aboard, however, the back pontoon had lost air. The rubber had a big gash. Razor rock, she thought. She would have to spend the night repairing the boat.

She found a campsite and set about sewing up the boat. The air was still. River otters played in a cottonwood trunk that lay in the shallow waters. The smell of mud filled her with joy. When I am alone, she thought, awareness is perfected.

So many years, season after season, she had been running this river. It had become as much a religion as any to be found in the world. She dozed off.

A kayaker appeared. "That was a hell of a run through Skull, Bodacious Rose."

"Cody, you caught me." said Isabele, jostled out of sleep. "I didn't see you there."

"Oh, I was there. I was watching from the Room of Doom. You made a fine leap onto the front of the boat. What I don't understand is how you managed to balance yourself through the hole."

With dignified pleasure, she replied, "I have the hooves of a caballo."

Cody pulled the spray skirt off the kayak and jumped out . "You know about the waterfall up the side canyon? It's about a half a mile from here."

"No. I've never been there."

"Do you want to go?"

She looked at him. The years haven't changed the sincerity in those icy blue eyes. "Sure, why not?"

"This may be the last time I see this waterfall," he said sadly.

"I know. We all move on." They walked up the canyon path. "Cody, why did you become a river ranger?"

"Well, I could say that I like the loneliness of the job."

"Come on, give me a better answer."

Upon further consideration, Cody spoke, "Take this waterfall for instance. It's pure water. It flows unobstructed, falling off rocks into pools of opalescent light. You can only reach this waterfall by boat. It is the only way to find this place, this Nature sanctuary that hasn't been rearranged into man's sense of order. It's a hidden paradise, perhaps one of the few that will remain as growing populations move into unsettled lands. The water flows as it has for millenia."

They walked through a thicket of scrub oak. Beyond, they could see the waterfall. Cody continued, "Viewed from below, water pours over the cliff. The azure sky wraps around this keyhole, blessed as if God's eye were peering through it. Its essence streams from the heavens. And yet," he paused and raised his arms up, "the sandstone canyon walls are testimony to raging war. Water against rock. A pathway to release its power, liquid has no boundary. Rock is its natural enemy."

Cody took off his clothes and walked into the pool. He took no notice of Isabele as he spoke again, "Water pushes upon rock in turbulent rifts, cracking and molding its prey into the most accessed pathway of movement. It becomes a predator that can move through its territory with purity. For thousands upon thousands of years, this war has taken place." He turned around to look at her.

"And now I am naked in the waters of this canyon. I experienced peace I can find nowhere else." Cody moved toward the white column of foam. The coolness penetrated his skin, which had been sweating in the heat of the day. "Element meets mortal. I, too, could become its prey."

At this moment, Isabele took off her clothes. She discovered what it was that she loved about this man. He saw the power of life. Magic ran through his veins. He maintained an innocence. Isabele felt that when she had stopped giving birth to children, the full feminine magic had stopped. In him, she found a new, vast purity. He knew the importance of spirit.

She entered the water. He took her hand. He pulled her beneath the falls.

They looked into each other's eyes. Their bodies moved toward one another. They wrapped their arms around each other. The water pounded their flesh.

"I shall always love you."

"It is I, who shall always love you."

TEN

Cody and Isabele never saw each other again. Cody moved to a small town on the western side of Wyoming. Isabele's three beautiful girls were growing into women.

Isabele and her husband were committed to their upbringing.

One day, while rummaging through some old papers, Isabele found a photo of Cody she had taken by the waterfall. She never did consummate their friendship that day. Her love for her husband moved her beyond the ephemeral moments of pleasure. She woke the following morning, opened her diary, and wrote:

> Your photo fell out of the pile.
> I picked it up with a smile.
> I looked at you, you smiled back.
> It's not wistful love that we lack.

From the diary of Isabele Rose Ranchera
—December 1993

EPILOGUE

Maria closed the diary. The women were silent. Cassandra broke the silence.

"Grandmother, that sure is a far fetched fairy tale. I don't understand the point."

"It's not a fairy tale," said Theressa Rose.

"It had to be. Mother was very imaginative."

"Cassandra, when your mother was a child, she used to write short stories and leave them in special places for me to find. She always loved my middle name. She told me that if the story were real, she would sign her name Rose. Look at the signature at the end of the story, Maria."

Maria opened the diary again. "Isabele Rose... What the hell!" A disturbed look came over her face. "What about the baby? Was he real?"

Gravely, Therresa Rose put her hand across her chest. "Yes, he was real. You children were too little to remember. It was a tragedy for her. She never talked about him. Your father respected her wishes." She looked at Cassandra. "So you see, Cassandra, there is magic around your mother. She was committed to your father."

The women got up and went into the kitchen. Their lives had been altered this evening, though they didn't know exactly how much or how to view this revelation. Both their parents had died. It was as if the women entered the lives of two people they knew a long time ago and now they had to relearn their parents' history as well as their own new history. No one ever fully understands the complexity of their relationships.

Each woman took a bowl from the cupboard and walked to the chili pot. A long sniff came from their noses as they poured chili. They brought the bowls to the table and sat. Food always had the effect of bringing together events of the day. They talked of the diary. After a while, Theressa Rose grew tired. She asked the girls to leave, for the reading had caused her great anguish. As they put on their coats, Angelina asked Meg to take special care of her. They gravely kissed their grandmother goodbye.

The kitchen door opened, and the night air flew in. The door closed behind the granddaughters. In the middle of the barnyard stood a coyote under the barnlight. The canine watched the figures walk to the car.

After they left, Therresa Rose moved slowly into the living room and sat in her chair by the fire. She picked up the diary. Tears fell. Darkness beckoned her into eternal sleep. Breathing in faint wisps of air, she dreamed of those golden leaves.

Velvet Hammer

"HOW DO YOU get downstairs, Grandma?" Bridget asked.

"I use walking sticks," Juliana said as she turned her head toward Bridget, "but, I haven't been downstairs for a week."

"Walking sticks?" Suzanne snarked.

"They get me up and down."

The girls all looked at each other. "Have you ever fallen?" asked Cassandra.

"Not once. Not one incident." Juliana paused. "I use the railing too."

"I really think you should reconsider my offer. The spare bedroom is on the same floor as the rest of the apartment," Suzanne urged.

"I told you. Give it up."

"What if you do have an incident? Is Violet going to carry you?" Suzanne continued.

"Violet watches to make sure I don't fall."

"Where does she stand?"

"Flight below me. Two steps away."

"Oh great. So when — not if — you fall, Violet is supposed to catch you?"

"I don't know. It hasn't happened yet. Now quit the third degree. I want to have some fun with you girls."

"I've got it," Cassandra announced as she got up and

stood with her back toward the bed. She patted her shoulders. "I'm going to carry you piggy back."

"Ooooh," the sisters cooed.

"I mean it," said Cassandra. She widened her feet so she'd have better balance. She patted her shoulders again.

"No, I'm too heavy."

"Naaah. Hop on."

"Hop on? What do you think I am, a mountain goat?"

"No. I think of you simply as a backpack." Her confidence sounded inviting.

A laugh came out of Violet who by now motioned the other girls to lift Juliana out of bed. But first, she carefully lifted the bed covers and looked underneath.

"Of course I'm dressed." Juliana snapped. She brushed the covers. "I've got some dignity left. I'm able to get pants on... most the time. And I'm not going to miss being as light as a backpack."

Bridget and Suzanne slid off the bed. They both moved Cassandra over with their hips. When they put Juliana's armpits in their hands and lifted her up a bit, Julianna let out a quiet fart. That got them laughing, which gave them energy to lift their grandmother. They helped her off the bed and onto the floor. Her knees gave way, but they caught her before she realized she was collapsing.

Cassandra squatted. "One two three..." her two sisters counted as they lifted Julianna onto Cassandra's back. Cassandra put her arms under Juliana's butt while straightening hefty thighs.

Julianna was up. She was wrapped over Cassandra's back like a threadbare blanket. The girls got her stabilized with incremental adjustments and stepped away.

"Are you sure you can do this?" Juliana whispered into Cassandra's ear.

"You are as light as my backpack. I got it handled," she whispered back.

Violet opened the door wide. Again, it creaked. Cassandra descended the stairs, one at a time with great agility. Very deliberately, she carried her beloved grammy. Juliana just barely hung on. She was not really pleased. When they reached the bottom, Cassandra stopped. She asked if her grammy was okay. Julianna nodded. That's when Cassandra took off, lickety split, galloping around the hallway to the living room, back down the hall and into the kitchen, whinnying as she slowed to a trot. Of course, Cassandra rounded each corner with some fancy hoof action. Now, everyone noticed there was a slight smile on Juliana. Cassandra stopped abruptly as though Julianna pulled the reins on her. She then gently lowered her onto one of the chairs around the table.

"Whoa my steed," Juliana chirped. Cassandra whinnied again.

The other sisters helped Violet prepare bowls of chili. They topped each bowl with cilantro and onions and finished with a dollop of sour cream.

"What do you want to drink? Suzanne asked.

"Beer!" yelled all three sisters.

"I'll go get it," Bridget said as she pushed the screen door open. She went to the car. When she came back with two six packs, Violet got the flour tortillas out of the oven. She was not going to let them get cold. She covered them with a cotton towel and placed them on the table. She motioned for the girls to dunk them into the chili. She forgot she had said this many times. She did not care. Nor did the sisters.

By the time the meal was finished, each of the sisters had drunk three bottles of Colorado Native beer. They were teasing each other about whose boyfriend or girlfriend was the worst in bed or the worst at keeping a relationship lively. Juliana had lost herself in the heat of her granddaughters' love affairs. She thought of her own love affair with her husband and her horse. She abruptly changed the subject.

"I'm getting cold," Juliana announced. "Violet, would you make a fire in the living room?"

Violet got up from the table, laughing at the girls' sorrowful tales of romance. She started to pick up the bowls and spoons, but Suzanne stopped her. She told her, "We sisters can clean it up."

Violet bowed at that, backed away, and turned toward the living room. The light in the living room danced with shadowy movement, a fierce fire being the main source of light. Violet turned on another lamp to soften the shadows' playful dances.

Julianna stepped cautiously into the doorway without any help. She then moved carefully toward the fireplace. The warmth made her shiver. She found her chair. Violet brought her a wrap and put it on top of her. The room was familiarly cozy in the sinking natural light. The granddaughters all pushed a plush chair around their grandmother, then made themselves comfortable, rubbing their legs back and forth like cats settling in for a snooze.

"Do you know why my nickname was the Velvet Hammer?" Juliana began. "Because you were always a smooth carpenter?" Cassandra teased.

"No, but that skill came in handy."

"Because you were a lounge singer and your stage name was the Velvet Hammer," Bridget guessed.

"No. Wishful thinking. I have no aptitude for singing. It's because I have been known to be patient... and be patient... and be patient... and then BAM! I strike people over the head with reality. And they don't even know yet, it's so smooth. And velvety. But they get it. They understand what I'm saying. I had that nickname mostly when I was running rivers. But I needed it several times for your grandfather. You'll find out. This journal is full of the Velvet Hammer's call to bring it down."

"I think we got the Velvet Hammer a time or two," Cassandra mused.

"Oh yes, you did! So, I have been thinking about what I want to leave you as my final advice." Juliana's eyes closed. Everyone waited. The fire continued to make shadows on the walls. The earth stood still outside as the winds stopped.

"I don't want to live much longer. I don't like feeling obsolete or desolate or left over. Whatever it is I'm feeling, I wasn't planning on living this long."

The beer suddenly lost its jovial welcome. The sisters knew this was meant to be the sermon of the century. They just wanted to know where the journal was, before she got sleepy. But Juliana had no intention of being sleepy until she got out her words.

"I heard your romance foibles. They can be that, but they can be so much more than you girls laughed about tonight. Look at each romance as a portal into knowing who you are. Don't be defined by anyone else — not anyone else's sense of importance or sense of shame.

"Fully embrace yourselves first. Take care of yourselves." Juliana stopped to catch a breath. "I mean it." She labored a few breaths. "I want you all to believe you can be strong and vulnerable at the same time. Strong is what makes you skilled to handle frustration. You'll need that skill indefinitely. But to always find your way back to each other, that takes courage. To be sorry. To say I've made a mistake. You're imperfect but you are wired for struggle. For survival. It's what hardens you into being practical. Being vulnerable is what makes you beautiful. Pay attention."

The girls bowed their heads. They knew in their bodies that shame had overtaken each one of them in its own way. It's what they cover up with humor. They just didn't get how being vulnerable makes them more attractive. She explained it a bit more, but let it go. It's not as easy to explain as years of living will do. She picked up the manuscript from under the chair.

"This may help to guide you. My vulnerability manifesto. My Velvet Hammer memoirs. I'm just going to read the first chapter and you girls will have to take it from there."

With that declaration, Juliana opened the journal to the first chapter. She cleared her throat and began reading. "Birth of the Dark Goddess..."

Birth of the Dark Goddess

EVERYONE IN BOULDER, Colorado, is born a god or goddess. Ever since the land was tamed, first by Indians, then pioneers, hippies and millennials, it has been a Camelot of the West. Those lucky enough to be born in this area frequently hear gasps of reverence from transplants paying homage to the native Boulderite. But no one can predict when a dark goddess of Boulder will be born. From the great unknown of the womb, where the alchemy of love takes place, a baby descends under the magic of the Flatirons. And it is the design of the omnipotent creator to decide who becomes a dark goddess, the messenger of the shadow side of love. These messengers are rare gifts to the human race. Yet, they are not necessarily exquisite earthly beauties.

She was both a messenger and a beauty. It's hard to explain what a messenger is. The tales of her life may lead the reader to one's own definition. Her life was fraught with real peril. In service to life, she made descents into the underworld of her subconscious. The hardest descents were either by horse, by raft, or by sword in order to receive the potent forces of new creation. She courageously surrendered to her own sacrifice in order to gain new power and knowledge of love... and the shadow side of love.

She was named Juliana. It was not her birth name. This name stood for honest benevolence. It stood for being creative under pressure. In emergencies, it stood for having intuitive abilities to resolve crisis or conflict. And yet, it stood for seeking freedom or opportunities to enjoy life, to make love, to go places, and have adventures. Finally, it stood for willingness to take risks to achieve these objectives. Her restless nature was insatiable for new adventures because each adventure made her desire another. She was honest and fair because she knew this was the only way to receive justice and honesty from others.

Her parents met on a blind date. There was no match.com back then. They had to meet in person, eyes to eyes. She was from Philadelphia, Pennsylvania. He was from Houston, Texas. She was the daughter of a candy store owner. He, the son of a civil rights judge. In back of the candy store was her father's gambling casino. Her extended family had to let go of three of their houses to pay off his debts. His family lost their anchor when late one night the judge was assassinated while sitting at his desk.

Theresa Rose Malara was twenty-five years old when she met her future husband, William Freeman Love. He was twenty-four years old with blond hair and blue eyes, an Adonis. Her black eyes and black hair caught his heart. Her beauty garnered the admiration of her brothers, cousins, nieces, nephews, uncles and aunts. She was a 1950s version of eye candy.

On her blind date with Bill, she told him she just obtained her high school diploma, going to night school. When she was thirteen years old, her parents insisted she quit school and work in the candy store because she could speak to customers in English. She spoke English better than anyone in her family of five brothers and parents who had immigrated from Sicily. She had been heartbroken to leave school. The underworld of the casino confused her.

She knew her only way out of poverty was to get her highschool diploma, to become educated. She was offered a two-year scholarship to any school of her choice in Pennsylvania. Her mother wouldn't allow it. She thought becoming a nun might be her only way out of this wormhole.

"How was your date last night?" Vincente asked. His accent was part Italian and part Philadelphia slang.

"It was really nice. We went dancing," Theresa answered.

"Where did you go?"

"We went to The Palace."

"Aaah faaancy!" Vincente cooed while chewing a bit of veal. The Italians managed to eat, talk, and gesture while sustaining frenetic excitement as long as meals were being eaten. "Did ya see that bee- u-tee-ful Marilyn Monroe? She's a knockout!"

"No, Vincente, she was not there." Theresa played along, always trying to speak the Philadelphia slang. She sounded more "educated," wanting to impress Bill. "But Gene Kelly was there. He asked me to dance. And did I show him how. He couldn't keep up."

Four brothers laughed. Four, because the fifth brother had died in the war. Bill smiled at Theresa. She caught his glance. Her smile back was part coy and part desperate. She didn't want her brothers ganging up on Bill. There was a forbiddance to their relationship.

'This girl has a sense of humor,' thought Bill. As he enjoyed savory bites of potato croquettes, blended creamy potato, rice and oregano with fried bread crumb crust, his thighs slowly melted together with hers — under the table where the mother could not see.

After the first course, her mother served a rigatoni pasta dish. As rigatoni slid into their stomachs, the conversation moved from latest girlfriends, to new babies, to the effects of the war, and to the future of their family business. At the end of the meal, the brothers patted their bellies to gesture that life was great even though they hadn't solved any of the world's problems. They were grateful to be well fed once a week.

After Theresa and her mother cleared the plates, they served a dessert of cappuccinos, bowls of almonds, grapes, and aged gouda. Everyone oohed and ahhed. Her mother brought out spumoni ice cream and sat down again. Then, Armand served up the next question, the inevitable query everyone knew was coming.

"Bill, what'cha planning for our sister's future?"

Theresa's heart performed a capriole. But, the brothers tightened up their bellies. They sat a little straighter in the chairs. Since Theiesa had no father — he had passed away when she was eighteen years old — the brothers each assumed his own understanding of fatherly duty.

So all their black scrutinizing eyes were now turned to Bill. And Bill managed to put out to the crowd, with great finesse, that he was as serious as he could ever be about a woman.

After many months of apparently sufficient scrutiny, Theresa and Bill married. Black and white photos of the couple portrayed them in their wedding attire in front of a Hollywood-style backdrop of a descending spiral staircase. She wore a bridal veil that swirled around her like alluvial wetlands. He wore an orchid in his lapel with a handkerchief folded into three triangles.

Unlike Theresa, Bill had lived with a great deal of freedom. After his father died, his mother went to work as a school teacher. Bill was five years old at the time and the youngest of three boys and two girls. No one coddled him. No one was really watching him. He could fly under the radar. At ten years old, he started to visit the town pool hall every chance he could get. He took to the cue stick like he had a fishing rod. His game was hot. He often said he had a misspent youth chasing snooker games.

When he was not playing snooker, he went fishing with his buddies. During the summers, from sunup to sunset, he was pretty much on his own. He learned to be an expert angler. A string of fish was greatly appreciated by his mother, who was raising five children on a teacher's salary. Whenever chicken was available, it was shared by six people. Bill sucked the juices down to the marrow of the bones, he was so starved.

By skipping two grades in elementary school, he was able to start at Rice University at age sixteen. He was on full scholarship. And with his athletic prowess, he was quarterback of the Rice University football team. By the age of twenty two, he had earned his Ph.D in physics and served in the U.S. Navy in the Pacific theater during the war. Now, his robust intellect led him to a teaching position at Penn State in Philadelphia.

Their blind date turned into a relationship. It was Theresa's mother's Italian cooking that enticed Bill to spend a lot of time with the family. He was initiated into the *famiglia* after he passed the loyalty tests each of Theresa's four brothers developed to scrutinize his intentions with their sister. Every time pasta was served, Bill was asked of his future plans and whether they included their sister.

"Bill, sit here, at the head of the table. you are our honored guest," brother Armand said. "Welcome to our Sunday feast." Armand pulled back the chair at the head of the table as he gestured for Bill to sit. As Bill sat down, a grin on his face widened. The spread of food on the table made him weak with anticipation. He waited for everyone to sit. Theresa placed herself next to him. The four brothers sat on the sides. Their mother sat at the other end of the table. She didn't need to hear Bill as she spoke no English. But she did want to see him in his Sunday suit. They all said grace, including Bill, who performed it flawlessly. "Pass the caprese," Anthony announced.

An oblong porcelain plate with rows of sliced homegrown heirloom tomatoes was passed down the table. On top of the tomatoes were slices of fresh mozzarella from the corner market. The aroma of chopped basil atop the mozzarella wafted to their noses. Olive oil and balsamic vinegar adorned the dish. They sniffed it as if it were tradition to do so. Bill salivated as the veal parmesan, the potato croquettes, the asparagus in a butter sauce, and the waldorf salad came his way.

"Who cooked this delicious meal?" Anthony teased. He said it in Italian. Theresa's mother smiled, her lips pulled in and her eyes closed. She enjoyed the compliments, feigning indifference. The ceremony of a well-prepared meal was natural to her. Theresa smiled as well, though she sensed the universal judgment that her efforts were second in merit to the matriarch's.

Theresa and Bill both smiled for their wedding photos. They looked eloquent in their completely groomed, yet somewhat uncomfortable stance. A stunning couple, all would agree.

When the first baby came, his parents were ecstatic. He was the epitome of Italian pride, the first-born son. The young couple showed him off, handing him from uncle to uncle. Bill took photos of him with his new camera. One day, while photos of the prince were being developed in Bill's dark room, he got exciting news. He was offered a teaching position at the University of Colorado in Boulder. They would move in the next couple of months, and as it turned out, never returned to Philadelphia.

Boulder became fertile ground for Bill's career. He was the hot shot professor who loved exploring the laws of physics through experimentation. His students were almost his age. For sport, he invited some students to the pool hall in the basement of the Faculty club. The hall had five tables.

In late afternoons, the place was jammin'. He played a few casual rounds with the president, chancellors, deans, professors and students. Martinis with an olive were the cocktail of choice, for he always had a bottle of Tanqueray gin in his locker. He soon gained the reputation of being a barracuda with a cue stick and a martini. Barracuda became his nickname. To live up to that name, he spent a lot of time in the university pool hall. This did not bode well for Theresa, who was already pregnant with their second child.

In the seventh month of Theresa's pregnancy, she found out she was having twins. The doctor said she needed to eat more because she had not gained enough weight even for one baby. But Theresa was influenced by all the dieting fads in LIFE magazine. She wasn't about to gain weight. Instead, she would prove to Bill's side of the family that not all Italians pop out babies and become obese. Bill encouraged her to eat for the health of the twins. She tried but could not respond sufficiently to his encouragement.

On September 11, 1955, Theresa had a C-section. The doctors didn't think she was strong enough to give birth naturally. They retrieved a baby girl and a baby boy. While Theresa recovered from surgery, the baby boy died. She learned this news when a priest came to her bedside to ask if she wanted last rites for her son. They had whisked the boy away before she could see his dead body. She was so angry she gave up formal Catholicism from that day on.

In her grief, Theresa could barely take care of the baby girl. Whenever she picked her up, Theresa started to cry. Her milk quickly dried up. Bill became deeply concerned. He bottle fed the girl every time he came home from the university. Even though Theresa could not form a bond from nursing the baby girl, she loved her deeply. It was not joyful love. It was dutiful love born of grief. And Theresa was completely dutiful in her ability to keep Juliana alive. Within three months of Juliana's birth, Theresa couldn't resist her giggling smile.

On Juliana's first birthday, Theresa gave birth to another baby girl. This girl was very pretty. She was healthy. She became the person who could make Theresa happy again. The family was complete. Three healthy, beautiful babies. People remarked that it was a miracle the two girls were born on the same day, a year apart. Theresa delighted in the twin idea — Irish twins, as the saying goes — or the replacement twin.

Two years later, in the Boulder Daily Camera, Theresa read an article about birthing twins. According to the article, doctors sometimes told the mothers one twin had died, when actually they would put it up for adoption. For cash. Her emotional well being declined precipitously.

Juliana had been born with great psychic powers. In order to survive the ordeal of her birth, she used her power to understand that what people were feeling was not necessarily what was being said. Her sister was not her twin. Her twin was a male spirit.

Theresa unconsciously doted on the older brother and younger sister, sacrificing Juliana's wellbeing for theirs. Juliana suffered under her mother's favoritism, subconsciously saddened by the injustice. Bill, however, took special care of Juliana. She became her father's baby. She became a student under his guidance. Her father admired his whole brood but she was "the apple of his eye." He always said, "Of all my kids, Juliana was born the happiest. She had the ability to overcome sadness and get on with it." Little did Juliana know that she would be tested over and over and over, repeatedly being forced 'to get on with it.'

The Tevis

AT 2:30 IN THE MORNING, the trail through the Sierra Nevadas was daunting. I couldn't see a damn thing without the moon. My headlamp was tucked away because Abu could see all. On either side of the trail, vegetation blended into the dark cobalt blue of the sky. The cool windless air amplified the silence. Only the pounding of Abu's hooves on dirt serenaded me. From the pounding, fine particles streamed up my nostrils, which have been caked with sweat, salt, and dust since the beginning of the ride, a day ago.

We started as 250 riders at 5 a.m. Trotting in single file through the forest, horses were riding up each others' asses. I had to pay close attention to the horse in front that might kick Abu in the flanks. We'd have to pull out of the ride. Now, we were spread out with miles between each other.

After 82 miles in the saddle, exhaustion prevailed. And yet, the trance of Abu and me, moving as one entity over long distances was sustenance. I told Abu, it's only us out here and we are the A team. He breathes, I breathe. He bends and twists, I bend and twist. He lifts an ear, I also listen for possible sounds of a predator.

Before the ride, I had called Otsie to see when he was flying to California to pit crew for Abu and me. He informed me that my father had died suddenly. When my sister told me he suffered a heart attack, I debated pulling out. But my father would have wanted me to compete. He admired everything about the sport. I sang some opera like he did and became lost in thought about the last time I saw him. My heart ached to distraction. I lost focus as my eyelids closed halfway.

Something was terribly wrong. I looked outward. Abu's neck was over the edge of a switchback. I almost reined the horse and myself over the cliff. Abu was poised to plunge but turned abruptly toward the switchback onto the trail. I'm almost hurled off the saddle. My feet hugged the stirrups. I quickly grabbed his mane and leaned upward, defying gravity and a near fatal mistake. The sound of rocks tumbling beneath us, quickened my heart. The sound grew faint as rocks hit the bottom 200 feet below. I placed my butt deftly back into the saddle. Trembling nerves quivered me up my back. I rubbed Abu's neck, which was crusted with sweat and dirt, to let him know, "Well done." Without urging, he continued down the trail. Giving up the rope, I laid it onto his withers. I had complete trust in Abu.

The blueberries and wild grape vines that line the trail smacked me in the face from time to time. The inner gorge was black now. No shadows, no trail. As we approached the bottom of the gorge, I heard running water. Dark became darker. My mouth opened wide. Rider and horse tumbling out of control played out in my mind. I screamed but no sound came out. We were about to enter water and I had no idea how deep it was. I tried to stay light in the saddle. Fear squeezed my legs into Abu's sides. He moved out a little faster, as squeezing was the signal to do so.

Believe! I saw the word written on the canvas of the night sky. Abu would get us through the blackest part of the canyon. His night vision was so much more accurate than mine. Harness the intelligence of the creature for its survival instincts. Sacred trust from human to horse is true unity. We were soaring into the darkness of the unknown. We flew into possible disaster. The sound of hoofs splashing through water cautioned me against hallucinations. In one leap, we cross the creek. I breathed deeply. Heaving rather, until I closed my mouth.

We moved out of the darkest part. Soon we approached the American River. Over the cliffs, the moon crested, casting an ambient light onto the trail. Abu smelled water. He picked up his head. As he was gaining speed, I kept the rope loose. Outlines of bushes and boulders appeared.

We moved as one living organism. Breathing in and out simultaneously, I held a steady seat. We were in rhythm. There seemed to be something dangerous about where that rhythm took us. I relied on Abu's superior instincts for over 6,000 sanctioned miles of Endurance Ride. We had ridden in all kinds of terrain, but riding along the American River alone at 3 o'clock in the morning in the middle of nowhere was way out there.

We came to the crossing at Poverty Bar. The river moved before us. The sweat of horses loomed over the water. Abu sniffed the sweat, tossing his head to move on. I pulled the rope halter around to keep Abu from entering. I relaxed in my seat, signaling to wait. I needed to look.

Across the river, just above the water were tiny green fluorescent glow sticks, strung from this side of the river to the other side, looking like small illumines that light up airport runways. About 200 feet across the water, the glow sticks ended. We were to cross the river within the boundaries of the glow sticks.

I waited, urging Abu to get a drink of water. Not a sound to be heard. Riders ahead and riders behind, but no one was close to us. It felt vast, the silence. The loneliness of my heart alternated with the attention to the trail. Other riders had met up with mountain lions along the trail, doing what they naturally do. Stalk! The river attracted a nocturnal game of predator vs. prey. Calmly, Abu sipped water. I took a water bottle out of my fanny pack.

Suddenly, Abu lifted his head, ears perked. He wanted to move out. He cautiously put a front hoof in the water. Finding and securing his hoof in the river bed, he put in another hoof. That hoof pounded the water, splashing cooling relief onto his chest. His back legs entered. Head down, Abu moved deftly over river rocks. Ambient moonlight couldn't help us through the black moving mass. Only tiny green sticks guided our passage.

Water came up to the stirrups. A few steps further, it came up to Abu's belly. The deepness was a mystery. Water came up past the heels of my boots. I lifted them up. Starting to float across the water, the current moved us diagonally downstream. Abu's astonishing agility excited the primeval, the ancient art of horse/man relationships. We were smooth as the river rocks underneath. We continued to float. It felt so serene, so comforting.

About four feet from the bank, Abu leapt out of the water onto the river bank. My torso absorbed the leap only inches away from his rear. I stayed in the saddle, only to be jostled again, as he shook off the water. The jostling roused me out of my lightness. At eighty-six miles, my thighs burned with fatigue, my feet swelled in the boots, and my lips were chapped like sunbaked mud chips.

This was the most extensive test of endurance I've attempted. Four straight years, I've been seduced by the Tevis. Without completing the last 3, I'm not sure why I tried a fourth.

Was I merely trying to define who I am? Why have I put myself through such physical suffering? If I got out of the saddle, my legs would collapse. 14 more miles to go. I summoned up more energy out of my thighs, signaling Abu to move out.

We reached the last vet check at Lower Quarry, 10 miles from the Auburn stadium. Having traversed 5 canyons, 21,000 feet of descent and 18,000 feet of ascent, completion was palpable. We started at five in the morning yesterday and it was three o'clock in the morning of the next day. 24 hours to complete 100 miles, the toughest ride I'd ever done. The end was sweetly in sight. And I was about to complete my first Tevis. My family would be so proud. The vet was looking the horse over for vital signs as I dreamed of victory.

"Your horse has the thumps." The vet called out as he put the stethoscope around his neck.

"What?" I asked.

"We're pulling your horse because of an irregular heartbeat."

I scream on the inside, 'N-O-O-O-O! This can't be.'

"When was the last time this horse got any electrolytes?"

Oh shit, I forgot to give the horse electrolytes at the vet check earlier.

"Sir, I have electrolytes in my saddle bag. I can give him some now. Please don't pull us. We can walk the last ten miles." The pleading in my voice was pathetic.

"The horse needs to recover."

"But, walking him will help him recover. I have two hours to go ten miles. We can do this! I promise I'll just walk him."

The vet hesitated. He and I both knew this was true.

And then I blurted out, "My father died yesterday. I found out while waiting for the ride to begin. I was going to drop out. But then I thought he would be so proud of me if I finished. This is my fourth try. And my last. I'm almost there."

The vet just looked at me. "We're still pulling the horse. It's for the horse's sake, not yours."

He was right. Completely deflated, I led Abu out of the vet's working space. We stood together in silence. How could I have forgotten the electrolytes? A small, but vital detail destroyed my chances of completion. Abu started to shiver. I found a blanket and put it over him. I rubbed his nose, massaged him across the withers and smoothed his tail. I pulled a tube of electrolytes out of the saddle bag and squeezed the paste into his mouth. He smacked his lips. The salt started to work on his heartbeat.

If I could just walk him, he would stop shivering. But what's the point? I looked into his tired eyes. "Abu, you have given me so much," I whispered into his ear. Abu put his head against my chest. I leaned into him.

"We have been through so many miles together. You have protected me. And transported us. I'm so sorry." Abu's eyes closed. Tears hung on the edges of mine.

"Why have you chosen me? You have given me unconditional trust. No one has ever done that for me. I remembered when you always reared up at me when I tried to get a bit in your mouth. You too were wounded. You trusted no human. And now, you were so powerful with the will of a soldier. I blew it for both of us."

The silence lulled me to drowsiness.

"Are you ready to go?" the driver asked. I opened my eyes to see a truck and trailer in front of me. Nodding my head, I walked Abu over to the trailer. He walked in. The driver closed the door and bolted the handle. I climbed into the passenger seat. Saying goodbye to the Tevis was a relief.

Maybe it's not about us. Maybe, it's really just about me trying to feel some sort of victory again. To stop feeling loss. To become realized in a different way. I come up short of understanding. Abu does what horses have done for thousands of years, traveling across animal trails for survival. Why do I spend so much effort running from my old wounds? Is that, too, about survival? Survival includes letting go of grief. But, you just can't will it. Doing adventure in order to take a bite out of life again is the game changer. The blessed life is lived, unattached to the past.

We crossed the bridge over the American River. Far below, I watched the moving black mass. Once again, sorrow rumbled. For my father. For my son. And now, for my horse.

ELISA LOVE STOWELL

The Fishing Vest

I DID A PAINTING FOR my father. After years of estrangement from one another, I thought I could appeal to his finer senses with an oil painting. On canvas, I drew my father in his fishing vest and waders in the middle of a mountain stream meandering through an aspen grove. I put a wash of paint over the drawing. The color sense leaned toward autumn. The brushstrokes were loose and slightly chaotic. The lighting revealed a majestic late afternoon tranquility. Silver snow capped the mountain peaks. My father had just hooked a cutthroat trout. I painted the trout in hues of the most beautiful Colorado sunset. It was my father's delight to hold one, admire its brilliancy and before the brilliance fades, let it go to swim another day.

When I presented the painting to him, he felt my esteemed regard for his passion. He spent many years on roads that lead to mountain streams across Montana, Idaho, Wyoming, and Colorado. Every trip was an odyssey to renew his membership in the 22-22 club. Membership is exclusive to fishermen who caught a 22-inch or more trout on size 22 fly, nearly the smallest size made. He also nicknamed the club "Tying and Lying" in honor of his buddies' tendency to brag about the size of the most recently caught fish.

Whenever he left for a trip, he put on a show of sorts. He strutted through the door to the dining room where we were sitting after a meal. He would be wearing his vest as though he were on the cover of GQ magazine. He unzipped every pocket and explained their carefully selected contents. He declared, with each item, how efficient it made him at putting a fly on the line in the middle of a stream. I especially liked his explanation of Gunk, and how the substance kept a fly afloat. When all his pockets were completely organized, he insisted, only then could he cast a line. As a teenager, I thought he was trying to tell me my bedroom should look more like his pockets before I go riding my bike.

Out of one pocket, he pulled out a plastic case and presented it as though it were a precious gem. In it were his latest harvest of hand-made flies. When he opened the case before my eyes, I stared at them like they were delicious little morsels, so feathery and sparkly.

If I were a trout, I would snatch these tasty appetizers.

By the age of fourteen, I began going with him to Gross Reservoir, in the mountains above Boulder, Colorado, to take a few fishing lessons. In the afternoons, after we each finished our school day, we drove up the steep winding road on Flagstaff Mountain. Winding up the steep curves for 30 minutes gave us time to do a recap of our day, our life.

He parked in the lot overlooking the reservoir. He would then sigh. He loaded me up with gear while he donned his vest. Each time he put on his vest, it looked more and more like a uniform. It made him look like an expert. Knowing that the pockets were perfectly organized, I thought he looked like an authority of western fisheries. It also made him look bigger than he really was. I examined the shape of its pockets. I counted how many zippers there were. His best flies, the ones that matched the hatch of the day, were hooked onto a piece of sheepskin sewn into the vest. The fingernail clippers attached to one retractable line, hemostats attached to another. I wondered how the fishing net could be comfortable when it sat in a big pocket covering his back.

Since my father was a physics professor at the University of Colorado, his casting lessons were infused with the physics of angling, how the action creates an arc of the line. He talked about the angle of the arm in relation to the rod and how it creates the degree of the arc. With a fish in tow, the arc of the rod becomes a parabola. He demonstrated how water refracts images by putting a glass water bottle with a straw into an eddy. The straw looked cut in half and slightly off line.

He taught me how to wet your hands before you retrieve a fish from a net because water's viscosity eases the friction between hands and fish. He also taught me to tie flies, but I had neither the propensity nor the patience for the skill. I admired them as art. His art. I especially liked how they looked on the sheepskin of his vest.

I didn't understand why all vests were beige. The sameness gave every vest the look of a uniform. I learned that beige blends with the aquatic surroundings. When a trout eyeballs the shape, it does not register as predator. From the perception of a fish, he may be a moose. Whenever he was a silhouette in his vest with the sun behind him, my father looked like a superhero with gigantic shoulders.

During these afternoon fishing trips, a gentleness passed between us. When we waded in the water, we were in the zone. No words passed between us. It was time spent, unwinding life events, a pause from the complications. We casted into the evening. We moved up and down the beach. Sometimes I borrowed flies from his collection after I couldn't untangle hooks from the brambles behind me. My back cast had no finesse. He restrained frustration after the third borrowed fly. He grumbled that he was going to have to make more.

I never caught any fish. Finesse never came. My father made it look so exciting when he reeled in a trout. But, I never found the patience to practice enough. Casting was hard and standing in a current just didn't jive with me. However, we learned from each other our love of water. He just liked much calmer water than I.

As I grew to be an adult, our togetherness drifted apart. He married again and didn't have time for our growing family. We still like to be in water. He liked meandering streams and I liked the rock and roll of white water. He did not understand my choices, either of water or self direction. I sought big water. The Colorado River in the Grand Canyon was quintessential paradise. Living on rafters for three weeks, under intense sunlight, and eating sand was bliss.

Fishing was eliminated in discussions between my father and me. Our conversations, surrendering to family matters, had the tone of seriousness, for years, due to the death of our son. He participated in his grandchildren's lives as well as he could, but his marriage to his second wife used up his time.

While I was working on the painting, my father had a heart attack. He was in the hospital for a week before I found out from a family friend. I was furious. How could he not want his family to be there? What was so painful that he couldn't believe we wanted to be there for his recovery. I hurried in my efforts to finish the painting. The image of him became the focus of my efforts. What was he really all about? Did I love him too much? Scientists are taught to face facts without any emotionality. Why can't I? Tears fell as I painted the color beige onto the vest. I made the shoulders bigger than his actual withering stature. I just

want to be with him as we once were when he used to take
me on his fishing trips.

He recovered. He became more appreciative of his
children and grandchildren. He no longer hoped to win the
big prize in physics. He still enjoyed the maze of equations
that progressed toward the fourteenth dimension. He
transformed from professor to friend. On one visit to our
house, he commented on what a wonderful mother I was.
He liked my easy going nature with my daughters. We both
agreed, his wife, my mother could never be this relaxed. He
started spending time with us again. The man I knew as a
child was emerging again. I think the death of his second
wife set him free. Our gentleness became familiar again.

A year later, he suffered another heart attack. He died. I
had really thought we could go fishing again. Instead, I took
his gear and his vest as part of my share in his estate. I
hugged the vest. Nothing hugged me back. He was really
gone.

For eight years, the vest lay somnolent under a pile of
gear in our boat room. It was just too strange to use the
tackle that stood for my father's identity. His soul still lay in
the flies he tied. His fingerprints still covered the hemostats.
His wader still smelled of his feet. I know this because each
river season I moved the tackle around to get to rafting
gear. I checked in with my father each time I picked up his
fly rod. I was not ready. I could not assuage my sorrow with
fishing. But I did often look at his painting.

It was only when I began to have heart problems myself
that I considered fishing again. Maybe my heart could sort
itself out if I could find a more relaxing sport. One day, I
pulled the vest out of the pile of boating equipment. It still
looked like his uniform. It was to become my own. I put an
arm through the shoulder. It was already too big. I slid the
other arm in. After adjusting the bulky fabric to my body, I
paused. It felt heavy. He really wore this all day long in the

hot sun? I rummaged through the pockets. There were three plastic boxes of flies. Enough to last me the rest of my life.

River season began again. We headed to the Middle Fork of the Salmon River in Idaho, the premier trout fishing area in the country. I had rafted with anglers so many times, I knew where all the great honey holes were. Trout ventured out of deep crystal clear holes to feed on flies, natural or artificial. It is not a chance event to hook a Rainbow trout. For years, I watched my buddies catch two dozen in less than an hour. It was now my chance to fulfill my legacy. I knew I had some good lessons inside of me.

Just above the Boundary Creek put-in is Dagger Falls. It is a seventy foot fall with house size boulders bordering the sides. There were pools in the boulders. Shoots of navigable water made it possible for the daring to run it in small boats. I simultaneously cringed and giggled while watching my kayaking buddies run the fall. It was kind of an initiation and set the mood of the trip.

Spectacular salmon jumped upstream against the current. There were hundreds of them, turning the churning water red. They congregated at different pools to rest. Then, a sudden leap out of the pool, up the fall to reach a higher pool. How powerful their physiques were to overcome the force of gravity and hydrodynamics. They maneuver through incredible masses to return to their spawning grounds. It is one of the most fervent instincts to procreate I have ever witnessed.

The put-in was challenging to negotiate. First, I rigged my raft in the parking lot. A cooler, a dry box, five-gallon water jug, dry bags, paco pads, river chairs and day bags, I strapped down tightly. When I cinched the fly rod case next to my seat, I felt like a bit of a phony, pretending I knew what I was doing. I put the vest into a dry bag. With the help of everyone on the trip, we lifted the raft onto a 100-foot wooden boat ramp. I climbed in the saddle. Everyone else pushed the boat down the ramp. One person held a rope wrapped around pillars to slow down the boat if it moved too fast. We all repeated these maneuvers for six other boats.

It was a delight to have hot weather on the Middle Fork. Many times we have rigged in the rain, rowed in the rain, eaten in the rain, set up tents in the rain, and fought to make a fire in the rain. Those journeys I merely survived, even in a dry suit. This trip looked like it would be more casual. Forecasters expected a high pressure system the whole time we were on the river.

Our flotilla of seven boats pushed off from shore. The first few miles are pure rock 'n roll whitewater. There was no let up of rapids. Only 500 feet downstream was the first hole. If you enter it sideways, you could be on the other side of upright. It was always a very stark wake up call. I had to stay alert. No daydreaming allowed. The eddies were fast. If my boat person needed to get to shore, she had to jump off while the boat was moving downstream. I cheered for my boat passenger who tied the boat to a tree in seconds.

In the late afternoon of the second day, my buddies pulled out their fishing gear. "Not yet," I whispered to myself. I was still whispering on the third day when Otsie took my gear and rigged the line with an elk hair caddis. He came to the campfire and placed the rod in front of me. There was no need for him to say a word. I took the rod over to my raft and leaned it against the rubber tubes. I hopped onto the boat and grabbed the dry bag. The clips easily snapped open. I looked inside and pulled out the crumpled vest. After a bit of shaking, I put it on.

The next day, at Sunflower hot springs, I found the spot, a deep lake of still water. Since I'm usually last in the flotilla, I arrived to see my buddies already soaking in the hot springs. This year I was going to skip the soak and fish instead. My boat partner took the oars. I told her to stay in the middle of this lake as I put on the vest and climbed with fly rod in hand to the front of the boat. I made the first cast with a whole lot of awkwardness. The second and third cast were slightly smoother. The line was whipping around with some finesse. I looked up at the soakers. We were going to be here awhile. For the next hour, we floated and fished.

The next two days weren't exactly relaxing. I had used up all the flies natural to the Middle Fork. They snagged on bushes. They flew off the rod when I whipped it too hard. They dropped into the sand. They stuck to the bottom of the river. Then I had to cut the line. One foozle after another. I ran out of patience as fast as I ran out of flies.

I did catch and release a few small trout here and there. My boat partner was overly enthusiastic about my catches. She knew this was a rite of passage and wanted to ease the pain. I pretended to curse the sport, but I was actually content. I loved fishing off a moving boat. It didn't matter that I had nothing to show for my efforts.

One lazy afternoon, while sipping a beer, I picked up the vest. Examining it more closely, I found sweat stains around the collar. The seams began to fray. The sheepskin lost its fluff. The nail clippers had rusted. My buddies wanted to taunt me. They wanted to find the expiration date on the vest. They wondered if I carried bobbers in any of the pockets. I had to act insulted. But I wasn't. I had my revenge.

The only elk hair caddis flies left in the case were number 22s. On the last day of fishing, I gingerly put one on the line. I could barely find it when I cast the line. I knew this was going to be merely casting practice. We stopped where an overhanging cliff cast its shadow across a relatively still pool, a relief from the sun. My buddies stopped at the same pool. It was big enough for four boats. We all lazily cast our lines. Their laziness was due to the exorbitant amount of fish they had caught in the past four days. They were satisfied. My laziness stemmed from the certainty that I wouldn't catch any.

My line suddenly grew taut. I yanked on the line to set the hook. It grew more taut. At this rousing moment, I stood up. The fish stayed on the line. Remarkable. I yelled into the air for anyone to hear "I got one!" They knew I was fishing with a 22. They looked from across the river. I started to reel it in. I told my partner to get the net ready. She put the oars up and looked for the net.

It felt really heavy. With my inexperience, an eight-inch trout felt heavy. I continued to reel. This was different. I could not see the fish in the shadowed water. The boat started to turn. I stopped reeling in. I let out some line instead. The boat swirled around. I looked tersely at my partner, unfairly, as she was not on the oars moving the boat. We were being dragged by whatever was on my line! The boat made a 360 degree turn. I maneuvered the line so it didn't get tangled under the boat. It turned another circle. I couldn't believe this. We kept spinning and spinning. From the laughter in my gut, a holler welled up and out of my lungs. My heart was elated. I had to see what this creature was. Cranking with strength, I turned the reel around and around. Slowly, the creature came toward the light. I still couldn't make out its shape. I told my partner to hold the net, that I couldn't possibly hold it. She moved the net under my rod, waiting.

The water was splashing furiously. She moved the net closer to the water. The audience yelled all sorts of suggestions. None were helpful. My rod now looked like a Roman arch. The splashes were mixed with a shimmering shape. Just a couple more turns of the reel. Up it jumped. A red flash! And down into the water again. I pulled up the rod. It jumped again five feet into the air. The red flash was three feet long and it was right up against the boat. My partner barely got the net underneath, when it spit out the fly, and jumped out of the net. Down into the depths again. Gone.

Damn! What just happened? We couldn't believe it. I had just caught a salmon on the smallest hook. My buddies watched with mouths open. They gawked. They had seen the size, but they insisted it was a trout. I insisted it was red. They said I couldn't have possibly caught a salmon. I retorted that I knew what color it was, and it was not the color of a trout. I had caught a salmon. The argument went on for days. Even months. But on one point we all agreed. I had become a member of the 22-22 club.

ELISA LOVE STOWELL

The Last River Trip

IT FEELS LIKE COMING HOME when the truck winds down the last switchback to the put-in on the Green River at the Gates of Ladore in northwest Colorado. It's October in the canyon. The golden orange leaves on the cottonwood trees against the maroon red walls are stunning. Josh parks the truck at the boat ramp so we can unload the gear quickly. Otsie and Alec need to do the shuttle. So we hustle to unload the equipment and blow up the boat tubes. The routine is as familiar now as it was forty-two years ago when my first raft trip started right here.

It's past river raft season. The place is quiet. A few cars perch in the parking lot, but no people are around. A girl parks her Honda with a boat frame on top near the ramp. She introduces herself as Desiree. She explains she answered a Facebook ad on a Western River Runners site. Alec had put a call out that he has an October permit. Desiree's new to river running, so she jumps at the chance to improve her skills, regardless of whom she's floating with. Then, she retreats to her car. Her keys are locked inside. It's quirky that someone would lock a car at this secluded place. It must have been an auto pilot move.

She is wrestling with the window, when the river ranger shows up. Otsie, ribbing, tells the ranger to put Alec through extensive gear inspection. Alec is a deputy sheriff in this area. The two men work together. Otsie loves to joke with law enforcement. I hear the three of them talking quietly about a rescue they made this season. Desiree interrupts the shop talk to ask the ranger if he had a door-opening tool. The ranger says he happens to have one. Watching the two work together to wrangle the lock open is like watching a mating dance between two birds. Luckily for her, they get the door open.

Later Otsie tells her, "He's single."

Desiree replies, "I noticed his hands. They're really soft looking. I go for rougher looking hands." This tells me something about her I can relate to.

This is our third or fourth autumn trip. We are beginning to see it as routine. Every year, Alec watches the allocation report from the Flaming Gorge water department. When they release water, he calls for a permit. Normally, this time of year, the river is too low for rafts, Now, the river comes up fairly high on the ramp. Perfect level for running, for the motto is "más lingua, menos dientes" or "more tongue, less teeth." Otsie has a t-shirt with these words on the front. He is compelled to explain what it means to every newbie on the river.

We have the boat ramp to ourselves, so we spread out the equipment. We can take our time organizing the gear. Otsie and Alec are on the shuttle run. Sierra lays out the tangle of straps. She organizes 100 straps into categories of length. I set up Otsie's cot and my tent. Dusk is moving in. I walk to the boat ramp to begin organizing.

"Assholes!" Sierra screams as she stands up from sitting on the tube. She and Josh have discovered holes in the tubes. She is vexed. Josh is too, though he shows no emotion. She is cursing Sage and Matt, who used the equipment for the Grand Canyon. Her reaction surprises me because of its ferocity. To Sierra, holes are the final blow, one insult too many on her list of her sister's irresponsible care of equipment: rusted griddles, mildewed pots and pans, duct tape patches, broken straps to river bags. I consider the list normal wear and tear. But I'm her mother, not her sister.

There are five ammo repair cans. We did not consolidate them into two before the trip. This adds to her frustration as she rummages to find the patch materials. She and Josh look over all the small worn out areas. They put on two patches hoping this will hold for the trip. They talk among themselves as they press the patches with a roller.

Nothing more to do after dark so we make hotdogs. We snarf them down and call it done for the day. Everyone needs to chill. The two hours it took to get from Idaho Springs to Eisenhower Tunnel, usually a thirty-minute drive, did nothing to help our moods. We should just climb into our sleeping bags and lay prone. I'm almost asleep when I hear Otsie arrive. It's probably around one in the morning. He is shivering as he slips into his bag. His bag is good to five degrees below zero, so it's perfect for him to be sleeping under the stars. The sound of the river lures us into a fitful sleep.

In the morning, I hear magpies trying to eat the breakfast muffins off the picnic table. l wake to Sierra yelling at the birds to leave our breakfast alone. Everyone is drinking coffee. Otsie throws a muffin on the ground for the birds so they won't attack the plate on the table. Sierra rolls her eyes and scolds her father. The sign on the table clearly says, "Don't feed the wild life."

"I'm not feeding the wildlife," he retorts. "They are clearly domesticated."

"Oh, so this is Otsie's interpretation of the sign," she remarks.

"Well, they're not bothering us, are they?"

More eye rolling ensues.

The frowsty smell from the outhouse motivates me to abandon my sleeping bag. The sun has already taken the chill out of the air. Unzipping the tent, the warmth hits my face. I stick my head out. The landscape speaks to my heart. I'm psyched to be here. This has got to be one of the most special places on the planet. Good morning, Green River!

I'm a little stiff from sleeping on a paco pad. I'm pulling my pants up when I realize the Ranger is walking toward our table. I apologize for my indiscretion. I go over to the kitchen stove and pour a cup of coffee. Sierra has already measured our rations of coffee as Otsie bought hazelnut coffee. Hazelnut is not real coffee, she says. So, she rations out the Guatemalan dark roast to last the rest of the trip because no one wants to drink "cozy" hazelnut. It's just not enough of a caffeine rush for this group. I down a couple of muffins. There's no relaxing until we push off.

I pack up my bags, tent, and tarp and take them down to the boat. A new day. A day on the river. Everyone should be in a great mood. Only they're not. Sierra and Josh have their boat rigged and ready. Otsie hasn't even put his cot away. He is moving slow. He is seventy years old. He should move slow. He is as slow as river time, which is fine with me.

I try to rig his boat for him. Sierra also tries to help but gets fed up when I just move gear from one place to the other. I've never seen so much gear. Extra cot, huge first aid ammo can, chairs, and tables. Not table, tables! Not only did he avoid sorting stuff to minimize, he deliberately took stuff because he could. This is an organizational conundrum so I have to wait for Otsie. The boat is going to weigh a ton.

By noon, everyone's rigged. We slam the oars into the oar locks. We push off. Four catarafts are on the water. This is the moment we have been working towards. Once we are actually floating, Josh asks Otsie for an edible. I take one too. Ten grams of THC. perfect buzz for river running. Today, we have Upper and Lower Disaster Falls. Nothing to worry about, we all agree. Desiree studies the river guide, but it doesn't tell her how to run a rapid. She has to rely on our experience. She takes an edible too.

Our boats enter the Gates. We are now officially on our own. I ask Alec if he brought a satellite phone or any other device. He shook his head, "No." So, whatever happens, we have to save ourselves. It's usually an exciting prospect, to save one's self. However, at sixty or seventy years old, it is more challenging than exciting.

When we are finally on the water, we put some distance between each boat. We can't hear each other. It feels like we are on our own floating island, like something out of a fantasy scene in a Japanese anime. We can do whatever we want. We can have a beer. We can have a smoke. We can row. We can giggle. We can talk smack about whomever. We can also be grateful to be here doing what we do.

The edibles settle in a slow, subtle way. Muscles relax into liquid. Water cascades. Shimmering and glistening reflections mesmerize. Colors heighten. All the sensations are pleasing until Otsie can't move the boat through Disaster Falls.

I look back at him in the captain's seat. With Otsie's titanium shoulders, I worry that he might pull the muscles from the metal. He is struggling. The oars are spaced too far apart to leverage maximum power. The weight of the boat is more than his capacity to maneuver deftly. The boat goes over rock after rock. Most of them are sleepers. But there is a decent size rock with a decent size hole in front of us. It is so obvious, I think Otsie sees it too. But he just goes right over it and gets hung up. He is so nonchalant that I am starting to get pissed off. He puts the oar in the downstream end of the hole. The oar emerges with water streaming through the newly chipped blade. I begin to have my doubts as to whether he can really row. He is a pro at reading water, but can he row this much weight? After

Disaster, I take the oars. OMG, the oars are way too far apart! No wonder. We should have checked this out before we pushed off.

We pull in at Rippling Brook, our first camp site. I'm a little unnerved by Otsie's performance. We unload the boat. The kitchen box comes off our boat. We need three people to carry the load to our designated kitchen spot. Once that's out, all other gear is easy to unload. Josh is getting something off our boat. While looking down, he mumbles, "Otsie's too old and you're too stoned to be doing this."

"Josh, you may be right," I say. I don't want to challenge him. I also don't want doubt to set into my psyche. We may both be too old to run rivers. The idea of self sufficiency is highly rated among river runners. Everyone contributes to the work equally. Everyone takes care of their own safety. But it is a team effort. The group is as strong as the weakest traveler. To bring Otsie along is a group effort. Is he the current weakest link? He would say, "Not me." But he demands everyone help him out. At any time. At any place. And I'm his sidekick. The resentment is building in Josh and Sierra. Their help is necessary, and Otsie taxes their patience. I'm jarred by Josh's remark. Instantly, I decide I'm not risking another edible. No one is going to blame my "poor performance" on being stoned.

Since it's October, sun shines between the canyon walls for about three hours. We need to get camp set up. Sierra moves the kitchen gear around to suit her. She gets the stove fired up. She puts dish water on. She gets the charcoal and the dutch oven heating. She is in charge. She moves like a chef in a professional kitchen. Alec lounges like a professional sitter, not budging from his chair or offering help. After I set up the tent, I ask Sierra what I can do.

As I am peeling a cucumber, I notice Josh limping. He looks to be in a lot of pain. When did this happen? I must have been at my tent. I watch. He is trying to carry equipment as he limps across the sand. The pain is too much, so he limps back to his cot. While he sits on his cot, I walk by and stop to make conversation.

"What happened?" I ask.

"I fell off the boat."

His toes are purple. "Do you think your foot is broken?"

"Nah, I think it's just sprained."

"Do you need anything?"

"No, I'm okay," he pinches a chew from his tobacco can and tucks it under his lower lip. "Elisa, I'm so happy to be on the river with you. It's so special to have this time together."

"Oh?" I hesitate. "I'm pretty entertaining, that's all."

"Yep, you are," and we both chuckle.

He sounds genuinely affectionate. 'What the fuck,' I'm thinking. He just insults me and then he compliments me. I'm confused. Bi-polar tendency, maybe. What we have here is a failure to communicate. This starts the beginning of a grand funk. His foot sprain is the catalyst. During dinner, he downs a pint of Knob Creek whiskey. He doesn't say a word.

Josh stares into space when he is not reading a book. When he doesn't want interaction, he reads. He reads a lot this trip.

We sit around the fire until it appears to be out, then throw some water on the ashes to make sure they're completely dead. When Josh tries to get up and walk, Sierra gets up to help him. She's very devoted. I'm no visionary, but I see Sierra's future. It has been my future. When you marry someone at least ten years older, who has always been accident prone, you eventually become their caretaker. For others this may not be true. But as she helps Josh hobble to his cot for the night, I notice a parallel fate. She's my offspring. It's in her DNA to be compassionate towards less-abled loved ones. His is a temporary disablement, but I feel for her.

"Sierra's a saint," I say to Alec from my river chair.

"Yes, she is," he agrees adamantly.

The next dawn, Otsie and Sierra are already in a tizzy. For years, Otsie always has been the first one up to put on coffee. They both like getting up before anyone else. I find them both snarling. Otsie doesn't like her coffee. Sierra doesn't like his choice of pancake mix.

I pour a cup of Guatemalan roast. She starts making pancakes.

"Did you even read the ingredients, Dad? There are no real blueberries in the mix. Why would you get this?" Sierra reads all the ingredients out loud. The blueberries were made of five different chemicals.

"I've gotten that pancake mix for forty years," Otsie rebukes.

"That's no excuse," she retorts.

Otsie's whole, rigid life is built on forty-year-old habits. Every motion, every action, and every reaction are foreordained. Sierra should understand that, but her lesson is, 'Why would anyone want to eat blueberry pancake mix when the blueberries are nothing but artificial chemicals?'

Ironically, she pours chocolate chips into the batter, which I find an equally disgusting ingredient for a breakfast meal. Really, chocolate chips? Some day, Sierra will be set in her ways. Maybe 'someday' is already here. But I'm just not saying anything.

While cleaning up, she admits she is uptight. I think the only way for her to be around us and Josh at the same time is to keep moving and avoid conversation. That's why she wants to be in charge of the kitchen. It keeps her from having to interact with us. With kitchen duty, she can avoid hanging around the fire pit — a river trip's equivalent of the office water cooler.

After her confession, I hug her from the side. "Practice

compassion," I advise. "He's trying."

"I know he's trying," she says, playing on the word 'trying'. "He's just so aggravating."

"Yes, I see that's how it is for you. If you practice compassion, it doesn't mean you are one hundred percent compassionate. And if you aren't with Otsie, that's okay. But practicing means someday you might get there. For right now, do the best you can."

"I am compassionate. I just can't be around him. He is so demanding."

"You already knew this. You have to learn to say No."

"He won't let you say No."

She is right. I know this from years of experience. He is the Guiltinator. So much for my lesson in Buddhism.

When I see Josh limp toward the kitchen, I warn Desiree not to attempt talking to him. I've learned over the years that this dude does not respond to anyone before noon. It's about nine in the morning. We have three hours to go before we can say anything. He drinks his Mountain Dew and a cup of coffee. And stares. I do appreciate his help to make trips happen and I always tell him so, but the staring wigs me out.

Breakfast is over. I start packing gear. Let's get on the river and enjoy the day. Otsie wants Sierra to help change the oars out. He asks her before I can blurt out that we can do this ourselves. She and Josh are already waiting on their boat. I start to undo the spare oars. Sierra gets off their boat and comes over. Otsie tells her she needs to get in the water. The sun is not in the canyon yet, so she is annoyed that he asks her to stand in the water and pull on the oar. The oar won't budge. She uses her might. No movement. I get the mallet and start pounding on the oar lock. By the time we get oars changed out, Sierra starts to shiver. It shows on her face. But she is so accommodating that I'm starting to feel like we are all taking advantage of her willingness to help, to be the organizer, to be Otsie's daughter, to be Josh's wife, and to be my daughter. I just want to have fun with her. To see her smile. Even laugh. She carries on so dutifully. I wonder if that's what the tattoo on her arm is about, the three-inch letters spelling ABIDE. As her mother, I don't ask. I know it's a private matter.

We push off shore. Another gorgeous day in the canyon. We float through Whirlpool Canyon in which the walls have become a black igneous fortress. There's not enough water to create those three foot deep suck holes, but we still get the feeling of a swirling tea cup at an amusement park. It's such a childlike, carefree feeling.

We come upon Triplet. Alec tells us someone died in Triplet this summer. It freaks Desiree out. Fear of unknown water plays with her head. Alec reassures her that these were boys messing around. They had such a fun run, they decided to run it again. They carried their raft back upstream, then made their second run through the "birth canal". This is a narrow passage of fast moving water that runs along the wall. Rafters usually avoid this risk, because the wall prevents a rower from using oars to maneuver. One of the boys didn't make it through the canal. Alec had to rescue the body.

We are last to set up for rowing through Triplet. Everyone else has had a smooth run. We do too until Otsie parks us on a boulder at the bottom. Otsie cannot row or push us off, so I try rocking the boat with my body. No budging. One of us needs to get out and push. Of course, 'one of us' would be me. I start to get out of the boat.

"Wait!" Josh yells.

I stop. He rows upstream. Sierra already has the throw rope in hand. She tosses it to our boat. Perfect aim. Otsie ties it to the chair. Sierra starts to correct him, then stops. I know what she's thinking, that we'll try it his way, then we'll have to do it her way. Otsie grabs the oars again. And Josh pulls. They pry our boat loose. Otsie unties the rope and throws it to Sierra as she is already stuffing it back in the bag. I clap at the perfection of the rescue.

Otsie says he could have done it without them. Of course, 'Narcissus' would say this.

We float downriver in and out of the shadows of the canyon walls. The sun will be directly overhead for the next rapid, Hell's Half Mile, one of the top ten drops in the United States. The anticipation of running this rapid still makes me need to go number two. It is the keyhole rapid to a more relaxing float. It is now audible. Desiree has been studying the map for awhile now, cigarette in hand. I don't think she is actually studying it as much as she is trying to assuage her anxiety. My exhilarated heart gets my attention as well. We are definitely scouting before we make the run.

Otsie rows to the left shore. I am ready with the bow line so I can quickly tie the rope around a tree. We glide into shore until Otsie gets stuck on a rock. This is getting ridiculous. I try to dislodge the boat by moving my butt around. Alec tries to help from his boat, but his feeble effort accomplishes nothing. I get out of the boat onto a submerged slippery rock. My feet slide into the deeper water and now I'm up to my chest in water. I am downright aggravated. Why is it that the guys are both sitting in the boats?

"Damn it!" I curse as I'm pushing the boat off the rock. "This is getting old." Otsie hears me but thinks my cursing is just part of the fun. Using the intensity of my frustration as a power thrust, I push the boat off. He sings me praises. Brother.

The sun is out in full force. I warm up quickly. I take the bow line and climb up the bank. I wrap it around the only tree there. This tree has probably held thousands of boats, groups of rafters puckered together to scout the rapid. Sure enough, from 200 feet upriver on the bank, the rapid looks scary as shit.

We study which way to go. So complex. Her eyes widening, Desiree starts to hyperventilate. "Do you want to take my boat?" she asks Sierra.

"No, I want to go with Josh."

They are standing together, taking apart the rapid. Sierra tells her she wants to get to the left of Lucifer's Rock. Josh signals Sierra that he's ready to run it. She leaves the bank. Desiree is in survival mode. When Sierra disappears, Alec and Otsie tell her she wants to go right of the rock. I weigh in, recalling that I've always ended up right of the rock. Desiree gets more hyped up. Two different ways to go. Does she trust the older generation or the younger generation?

Does she listen to youthful vibrancy or years of experience?

"It looks complicated," I say, "but it's not. Take it in sections. Once you get around that top rock," I point as I'm explaining, "pivot your boat around and row backwards toward the other bank. Don't try to push. Pull into the eddy there. It gives you time to maneuver. See how it moves to the right of Lucifer? If you go left, you go against the natural pull of the hydraulics. It's a puzzle from here, but when you're in it, you will know what to do."

Here come Sierra and Josh floating slowly into the tongue of the rapid. We want to watch their run, so we scramble to a better vantage point. Desiree watches as though her life depends on their success. Her anxiety grows while waiting for the slow water to take the first boat to the top of Hell's Half Mile.

With Otsie's record of landing on rocks this morning, I have my own anxieties. I'm preparing myself for a swim.

Sierra and Josh start floating swiftly down the tongue. Josh pivots around the top rock. I think he is trying to go left but the hydraulics take the boat right. We can't really tell what they are trying to do. He is working hard on the oars. It's obvious they didn't intend to be where they are. The boat turns sideways as the river takes them right over the center of Lucifer. Then, the boat drops and stands on edge in the hole below Lucifer. Sierra is about to go under the boat, when she climbs effortlessly to the high side. Josh is still on the oars. The crest of the wave lets up and their boat comes out of the hole. We watch as they continue downstream. They temporarily stick on some minor rocks. Then, they're out. The whole run happened so fast I didn't have time to worry about my daughter getting stuck under a boat in a large hole. So much for the millennial advice. Desiree is getting worked up.

"Do you want to take my boat?" she pleads with me.

"No, I don't know your boat."

"I don't think I can." Her voice is shaky.

"It looks complicated and nasty. Once you're in it, the water takes care of you," I reiterate.

"It didn't take care of Sierra and Josh."

"Because they went against the natural flow of the rapid."

It's her turn to run it. I'm feeling sorry for her. I know she's not going to get hurt, but she doesn't. "You got this Desiree. May the force be with you," I say with some levity. She doesn't seem convinced or relieved. She wants to smoke a cigarette. As she and Alec leave to do their runs, I watch her. I'm beginning to appreciate her authenticity.

Otsie is somewhere, watching. I wait. And wait. Maybe I should find Otsie. No, I don't want him to make fun of me right now. He preys upon insecurity. Being tossed in the cold water at sixty years old would tax my heart. As I'm talking my heart into taking on a blast of cold water, here comes Alec's boat.

Nice start. Good pivot. Pull back. Pull. Pull. Didn't pull back far enough. Ugly, but he got to the right. He's in the clear. I look upstream. Here comes Desiree. Her boat is looking good. Looking good some more. Pulling back.

Around Lucifer. Amazing. Clean run! She needed that to build her confidence.

Otsie's done this run at least sixty times. He is great at reading water, but I'm worried that two titanium reverse shoulders can't pull this pig boat across the eddy. Otsie climbs into the boat. He is humming a tune. It irks me that he seems so *laissez faire* about this. He sits down and looks around for any loose gear. I unwrap the rope from the tree, roll it quickly, and stuff it into a safe, accessible place. We push off. We move slowly. The tongue grabs us. We move faster. The sharp rock is to our right. The water moves swiftly. Otsie starts to pull back. That was smooth. Pleasant surprise. 'Pull. Pull. Pull,' I say to myself as though my unspoken directions will add to his titanium-restricted strength. We are just on the right side of Lucifer. Smooth. He straightens out the boat. We miss every possible hang up. How did he pull off a run like that through Hell's Half Mile?

"Nice run!" I smile as I look back at him.

He has a shit eating grin. "Don't I get style points for that? Huh? Huh?"

"Yeah, babe, you get style points for that beautiful run."

"Más lingua, menos dientes," he sings.

He's still grinning as he dodges all the rocks in the "Teeth Garden" below. I feel proud of him. And relieved for me. Everyone is through Hell's Half Mile. I notice movement in the bushes. Sierra dashes into some brush, now that she is satisfied of our safety. We see Josh waiting in the boat as we pass by. Later, he comments how long they were waiting for everyone. I can't let this latest complaint add to his litany because Hell's Half Mile always takes awhile to get boats through.

"Seriously dude? If you had actually flipped, there would have been no one to rescue you. And the potential was definitely there. Lighten up on us." He's acting like the most competent guy in the world. Getting through the rapid safely is the goal, not getting through it in five minutes.

The rest of the afternoon is the best time for Otsie and me. We don't think about anything: our past, our future, money. We just laugh. And we high-five our run through Hell's Half Mile. Steamboat Wall is in sight. It's tradition to kiss the wall as we float by. We slow down. The tips of the pontoons are an inch from the gigantic wall. I lean over the edge of the frame.

"Get a little closer to the wall, Otsie" I start to pucker. The water is just a little too fast. I don't want to scrape my lips and leave part of them on the wall. "Slower, slower..." I put my hands on the sandstone. My lips meet the sandstone. Now KISS! A smack on the wall from my lips. The tradition carries on.

We camp at Wild Mountain. Calm permeates among us. We are laughing at ourselves around the campfire. The next day is an easy float as it's only a couple of hours on the water if we camp at Jones Hole. We do wonder where Josh is going to stop for the night. Is he going to pass Jones Hole? Is he going to run Island Park? We have no idea. The self-appointed leader is in some parallel universe of communication. Whatever plot he's got, we don't have a clue. And we don't care. We are grooving on the water.

From a half mile away, we can see their boat parked at Jones Hole. Josh is showing consideration for us. We are now camping at Jones Hole One, the best site out of five possibilities. This is my favorite place on the planet. After we set up camp, Desiree and I walk up the creek. Desiree is relieved to have the rapid behind her. She tells me that she's glad I forced her to do it. I did no such thing. She should be willing to do any rapid if she's going to do this sport.

There's a fish hatchery twelve miles upstream. Sierra goes off to look at fish as she is about to complete her Ph.D dissertation on fish genetics. The guys are probably sitting around camp. I'm bragging about Otsie's run. Then, we walk in silence for a while. Whenever I walk up Jones Creek, I imagine the first people who might have inhabited this place. Did the area have enough resources for people to survive? Did they cultivate food here? Did they make babies here? Were there enough elk and deer to hunt? We find a rock to sit on and watch the fish in the pools. It's too late to walk up to Ely Falls.

Getting an early start in the morning is key to rowing through Island park. Afternoon winds blowing upriver make it difficult to row through languid water. We try to wait for the sun to hit the water before we push off. Josh needs to be at work the next morning at 6 a.m. No time for dillydallying. For years, Otsie had to be at work early the next day as well. He used to bang pots and pans to get everyone up at 5 a.m. or bring coffee around to each tent. You never knew which method he would choose. Neither method is Josh's style. Nor Sierra's. She just hustles us along through hazelnut coffee, and she's right. It sucks. Through breakfast, through clean up, and through camp dismantle, I appreciate her style. But Otsie is oblivious to subtlety. Sierra finally starts taking gear from where Otsie set up his cot. She brings the gear down to the shore and places it next to our boat. I watch her as she walks up the hill again. She is now going to pack up the groover. She doesn't even say, "Last call!" That speaks clearly to me that she wants to get this geriatric show down the river. She brings the boxes to shore. There is nothing else she can do so she sits on the boat while Josh assumes an excruciating pose of impatience. He is very transparent though. I sense a seething start for the day. Would-be leaders need to learn how to hold their cards closer to their life vests.

We do get an early enough start to avoid afternoon winds through Island park. I am rowing with no let up through meandering water. There are many channels that braid around small islands. It's difficult to choose the right channel that won't get us hung up on a sandbar. We enjoy the mystery. The air is absolutely still, which is rare. After three hours, I am still rowing. Josh, Sierra and Desiree are up ahead. Alec is behind us. He has the permit, so as long as we are ahead of him and constantly rowing, we are satisfied that we are doing our best to keep up. Who couldn't delight in the savory scenery? It's so delicious. Tangerine cottonwood leaves against a turquoise sky. High desert hills with Cedar and Pinion trees. Hazy canyon walls. Simply stunning. Why wouldn't Baby Boomers want to go on river trips? But we don't have time to relish. The frontrunners are far out of sight. The millennials rule.

We see the boats parked at the campsite before Split Mountain. We also see a couple of trucks. When we arrive, Josh is ready to leave.

"No time for lunch?" I ask.

"Sierra and I have already eaten lunch," he says, "and we took a nap."

So much for playing cards. We sit down at the picnic table provided for day campers. Otsie sees elk antlers in the back of a truck and starts to talk to the hunter. His friendly chatter is irking Josh. He has to leave. He walks down to the boats. An already long day is becoming longer with Otsie chatting up a hunter. We finish our canned sardines and walk toward the boat. Josh is sitting in his boat. As Otsie walks down the ramp, he suddenly decides he needs to relieve himself. When he turns around to use the public restroom, Josh starts into a rant. Sierra is caught between her regard for both men. She tries to placate Josh. I can see her whispering. She starts to massage the back of his neck. I don't think that will work this time. We are not trying to be deliberately slow. I hope he understands this. Our boat naturally floats more slowly than theirs. We have a lot more gear. Superfluous gear. Old people's gear. Guilt is starting to invade me. I should have looked over the gear. Slimmed down the load. But nobody in the group properly assessed our gear before the trip. No one blew up the tubes. No one checked the rusted out clamps on the hand washing part of the groover. No one consolidated ammo cans. It's a group effort. Guilt does not last long. It's either everyone's fault or no one's fault. It's how your outlook on life sways.

Split Mountain is a sequence of fun rapids. Nothing is technical. It's a great ending to the trip. I enjoy rowing Otsie through the rapids. When he is relaxed, he becomes more lovable to me, so I want the memory of him on the front of the boat to become etched into my heart. We are near the end. We see mountain sheep grazing near the river. We see the familiar curved strata of rock that mark the take out. I'm feeling nostalgic. We have taken many groups of people on many rivers for decades. People remember those trips as being among the best times of their lives. Water heals. So, I'm confused. When are we too old to keep doing this? I just don't know. With eighty-six years of river running between us, we've had zero drownings. It's a bizarre measure of success, but a meaningful one.

The shadows on the water tell us it's about five in the afternoon when we arrive at the take out. We are going to pull up next to the boats. Their boat is already unstrapped and equipment free. Sierra is rolling a tube in the water to clean it off. Josh is carrying gear up the ramp Desiree is parked next to them. She is smoking a cigarette. The scene seems casual but we know it's not. I start to unstrap equipment as we are drifting towards the ramp. The end of a river trip is usually a joyous occasion. Music usually booms out from the trucks parked by the water. Beer drinking happens. People are hugging and laughing while gathering up equipment to put on the trucks. Not this time. There is a menacing sense that we are inadequate in our ability to get the job done quickly, so we can escape before the atmosphere deteriorates more. Alec doesn't let this get to him. Desiree doesn't know us enough to feel the unspoken strain. Body language speaks volumes. It irks the shit out of them that we are trying to keep it easy going as we keep moving. What plays through my head is that we did not pose any danger to the group with our senior moments, our snail's pace, or our rowing. Let's be honest. Isn't this what really matters?

It is a sentimental moment when we pull out of the parking lot. Memories of past river trips conjure up Grandpa Otsie II and other wonderful people who became so connected to each other on our trips. Otsie's father was seventy-four when he did his last trip with us. He was to row the micro on the Middle Fork of the Salmon River. At the put-in, Grandpa Otsie fell onto a rock in the water while pulling his boat down the ramp. We wanted to take him to the hospital, but he insisted on being on the river. He ignored our pleas. Yet he couldn't row because his ribs hurt so much. Pain was constant. Someone else had to take his boat. I had to row alone. My boat partner, Cassie, needed to hang onto him on his son's boat. Through the rapids, he was swaying to and fro because he was on painkillers. By the second day, he was spitting up blood. He had to sleep in our tent because he was so disabled. I even had to help him get dressed. We all took care of him for six days. Nobody begrudged the care, even though we knew he shouldn't have been there. At the end of the trip, we took him to the hospital in Salmon, Idaho. He cracked five ribs.

Nobody talks in the truck. Otsie puts on an audio book. So silent. So not what an ending to a river trip should be. We are all accommodating Josh's anger with a mutual moratorium on laughing. His anticipation of lack of sleep before he goes back to work is gnawing at him while he drives.

We pass the "Welcome to Colorful Colorado" sign. The

desert at dusk is colorful in its subdued hues, but I don't comment. So many miles to go. We pull into the Kum and Co gas station in Craig, Colorado. Everyone gets out. Otsie fills the tank. We all use the restroom. I am waiting for my turn when Josh comes out of the restroom. I don't look at him. When he goes to open the door to the truck, the keys are locked inside. Thank God I miss that pissed off moment. Otsie has a spare. We all need something to eat before we do the last leg of the trip. Josh wants to go to Taco Bell. We pull up to the fast food joint. It's gone out of business. This adds to the tension. We pull up to Wendy's. Josh orders first. We decide to sit at a table rather than eat in the truck. When he opens up the paper to his hamburger and takes a bite, he grimaces. He undoes the hamburger and looks at it. He tells me he has my order. "No," I say as I point to Otsie still placing our order at the counter. He slams the burger down onto the paper. He shouts out an expletive. Sierra and I don't look directly at him or at each other. He crumbles up the paper and hamburger, throws it into the trash and leaves. I see him sitting in the truck as we all try to snarf down our food.

When is this going to end? Four people who love each other in our own peculiar ways are paralyzed by frustration and familial obligations. Are we just too much for each other? l really don't understand the wellspring of our pain. I guess we just need to drive home and call it a day. I do know this is our last river trip together. They have forgotten how they got here. How they learned these river skills. It's not like we just showed up and asked for a free ride down the river. This has been a cooperative exercise in life since Sierra was five years old.

We drove through Steamboat Springs, Rabbit Ears Pass, Kremmling, Silverthorne, and Eisenhower Tunnel in silence. I didn't raise my daughter to live in constant need to psychologically pivot between family members. Or maybe I never really noticed her inner rage. We are constantly dancing around Josh's silent rage. I want to confront our pain, but I suck it in.

Our children pass through us. And for a time, we give them a childhood we wanted for them. We give them adventures to develop life skills. We give them boundaries and opportunities. We give them more and more freedom to explore on their own. People sometimes call Otsie and me "figure-it-out parents". Helicopter parents, we are not. So, they can become the water moving over and around rock.

THE END

About the Author

Author and artist Elisa Love, born and raised in Boulder,
Colorado, began river rafting as a teenager. She moved to
New York City and worked as a scenic artist for several
theatrical productions. She moved back to Boulder, married
Otsie Stowell, and gave birth to three children. Their son
died after a year of overwhelming health struggles. The
couple began taking their two daughters rafting almost as
soon as they could walk.

During the 1990s, Elisa began her second career as an
elementary school teacher in Boulder. After retiring from
teaching she and Otsie moved to Livingston, Montana,
where they still live and create works of art.